"I want to t

Mollie didn't struggle to avoid his touch. She seemed held in place by some magic spell, helpless to resist. She drew in her breath as Pearce's fingertips touched her jawline, rose slowly and traced first the line of her eyebrow, then the silky line of her cheekbone.

The emotions that Mollie had been trying to freeze suddenly thawed and flooded her tired body. The feeling she had tried to stifle since she'd first stepped on the plane broke free and stormed her tired mind.

It feels so good for him to touch me, she thought dreamily.

His hand moved to frame her jaw, and he tilted her face toward his. "Your mouth," he said, bending nearer, "is like your voice—mysterious. It takes special investigating. May I?"

Then he did what Mollie had secretly wanted him to do from the moment she first saw him with his dark glasses and his fascinating, unreadable mouth.

Pearce pressed his lips to hers and kissed her as she'd never been kissed in her life.

Bethany Campbell, an English major and textbook consultant, calls her writing world her "hidey-hole," that marvelous place where true love always wins out. Her hobbies include writing poetry and thinking about that little scar on Harrison Ford's chin. She laughingly admits that her husband, who produces videos and writes comedy, approves of the first one only.

Bethany recently received the 1990 Maggie Award for her Harlequin Romance #3062 *Dancing Sky*. It's just one of this talented author's many romances to have delighted readers around the world.

Books by Bethany Campbell

HARLEQUIN ROMANCE
3000—THE LOST MOON FLOWER
3019—THE SNOW GARDEN
3045—THE HEART OF THE SUN
3062—DANCING SKY
3079—THE ENDS OF THE EARTH
3109—EVERY WOMAN'S DREAM
3133—THE CLOUD HOLDERS

HARLEQUIN INTRIGUE
 65—PROS AND CONS
116—THE ROSE OF CONSTANT
151—DEAD OPPOSITES

Don't miss any of our special offers. Write to us at the following address for information on our newest releases.

Harlequin Reader Service
P.O. Box 1397, Buffalo, NY 14240
Canadian address: P.O. Box 603,
Fort Erie, Ont. L2A 5X3

EVERY KIND OF HEAVEN
Bethany Campbell

Harlequin Books

TORONTO • NEW YORK • LONDON
AMSTERDAM • PARIS • SYDNEY • HAMBURG
STOCKHOLM • ATHENS • TOKYO • MILAN

ISBN 0-373-03163-7

Harlequin Romance first edition December 1991

EVERY KIND OF HEAVEN

CHAPTER ONE

SIX MONTHS AGO, when Mollie first joined the cast of the soap opera, the woman who played Dr. Katherine Bleekman had taken her aside and warned her.

"This place is crazy," she said. "You never know what's going to happen next. But I'll tell you one thing. If the director *ever* wants to see you in his private office—look out. You're in trouble."

"Trouble?" Mollie echoed warily. She'd been happy to find a job at all.

"In soap opera, you never know what's going to happen to your character," the woman said, a fearful grimness crossing her face. "The writers might do something *terrible* to you—with no warning. They're famous for it on this show. Somebody's always getting called in and told it's all over." She drew her finger across her throat, a sinister motion.

Since their talk, four actors had been called into the office and told their characters were to be killed or otherwise eliminated. Among them was the woman who played Dr. Katherine Bleekman. Dr. Bleekman was unexpectedly killed by the bite of a deadly Gaboon viper planted in her apartment by her rival, the evil Dr. Sebastion Forest. Shortly after, Dr. Forest met with a freak scuba diving accident and was also written out of the script.

This time it was Mollie who'd received the dreaded summons to the director's office. She sat uneasily, waiting for him to stop pottering about with his cold medications and tell her why he had called for her.

Maybe it's not that serious, she thought. *Maybe I'll only be lost at sea for a while.... Maybe they'll decide to fly me to England for emergency brain surgery, the plane will go down and I'll just disappear for a few months. Or they'll just give me amnesia. Or maybe lose me at sea and give me amnesia, too, but let me come back, good as new. That wouldn't be so bad.*

Outside the snow drifted down between the gray buildings. In the office, however, the air was warm and humid from the spray of a steamer beside Leon Medvett's desk. The room smelled of menthol and eucalyptus. Leon had a cold, and he brought as much melodrama to his suffering as he had ever brought to the soap opera he directed.

He coughed. He sniffed. He smiled gamely. "I'll be frank, Mollie," he said. An expression of pain crossed his face. "We're killing your character. The writers are pulling the plug on her life-support system. We're letting her die with dignity."

Mollie didn't flinch. She kept her legs crossed nonchalantly, her chin high, her gaze steady. She vowed to seem calm, even debonair about the whole disaster. She was, after all, an actress.

"The writers decided to kill you during the holidays." Leon ate a vitamin C tablet, then blew his nose. "You know, to crank up emotions. It's nothing personal. I myself feel very bad about it." He began to sneeze.

The only sign of emotion Mollie showed was to straighten her spine. *Drat,* she thought. *Getting killed. This puts a crimp in my wedding plans.*

She gave a complacent one-shouldered shrug to show she understood and accepted what Leon said. For the last six months she had played the character of Clarice on the daytime drama "Doctors' Hospital." For the entire six months Clarice had been in a coma. She had not moved or spoken or so much as groaned. It was not, in short, a challenging role, but it was a job, a genuine acting job, and the salary had paid the rent.

"Gesundheit," she said when Leon stopped sneezing.

"Sorry to do this so close to Christmas," Leon said, sniffling into a handkerchief. "But the writers thought it would be more dramatic. You know. We've had Christmas weddings and Christmas babies before this, and Dr. Finlay's house burned down one Christmas, and we've had a few Christmas deaths and accidents, but we've never pulled anybody's life-support system on Christmas. What emotion! It'll be a first."

What Leon said sounded both monstrous and heartless to Mollie, but she nodded, trying to look as cool and professional as possible.

She was not a glamorous woman, but she was an arresting one in a wholesome, breezy way. Her strawberry blond hair was long and luxuriant, and she wore its tumbling waves pulled back, fastened with a barrette. The delicate sweep of her auburn brows emphasized her wide blue eyes and the dramatic line of her freckled cheekbones. She knew she was no great beauty, but she had a well-trained body, an expressive face and a husky, versatile voice.

She had always known that she would have to rely on talent and drive to succeed, not prettiness. What she hadn't realized was how much an actress also had to rely on sheer, unpredictable luck. Her luck, like that of the hapless character Clarice, had just run out. She was about to be jobless.

"So," Leon said, examining a box of cough drops, "we'll be using you for another two weeks. Then you're free. I hope you find rewarding work. I happen to have a lot of faith in you. I believe you can play much more challenging roles than a woman in a coma."

"Thank you very much," Mollie said and smiled mechanically.

"And in any case," Leon said, putting his cough drops away, "didn't you want time off at Christmas to get married?"

Mollie nodded. "Yes," she said, keeping her cool smile in place. *But I didn't ask for eternity off,* she thought darkly. *Michael isn't going to be happy about this. He's already worried about money and how we'll survive. Thanks a lot, Leon. How would you like it if somebody killed you off for Christmas?*

"Well, there you are," Leon said. "You can take as long a honeymoon as you want. You're taking a honeymoon?"

"Yes. New Orleans." *If we can still afford it—now that I'm jobless.*

"Ah," Leon sighed. "New Orleans. Sunshine. Palm trees. Warmth. The French Quarter. Jazz. I envy you. I envy you everything. Your youth. Your health. Without your health you've got nothing." He sneezed again, this time with such force it brought tears to his eyes. He looked at Mollie, his nose red and his eyes brimming with moisture. "You're blessed, you know that?" he said, in his raspy nasal voice. "Blessed."

Blessed, thought Mollie darkly. Right. Blessed were the unemployed.

IT HAD TO HAPPEN, she kept reminding herself as she trudged to her apartment through the falling snow. She had always known that those bloodthirsty ghouls, the writers, would probably not let Clarice survive. The writers didn't care about actors. They cared only for the intricacies of their story and the amazing surprises they could spring.

With the greatest abandon they killed off characters or lost them on safaris or in avalanches or in foreign revolutions; they gave them amnesia or multiple personalities and dealt out thousands of afflictions, physical and mental. No, Mollie thought, pulling her muffler more tightly about her throat, it shouldn't surprise her that they were killing Clarice.

She had hoped, however, that Clarice would endure for at least another three or four months. She and Michael were getting married at Christmas, in two weeks, as soon as Michael finished the course work on his master's degree in drama.

It was to be a small wedding, without fanfare. Michael would come to New York from Minneapolis, and they would be married by a justice of the peace, not announcing it until afterward. Mollie didn't even have an engagement ring; they had decided it was an unnecessary expense.

The one luxury they were allowing themselves was a four-day Christmas honeymoon in New Orleans. Mollie had already bought the plane tickets so that she could get the discount for ordering early. They were tucked in their special envelope and hidden safely in a kitchen drawer.

Michael said that he had always dreamed of going to New Orleans, and Mollie, after a lifetime spent enduring the long cold winters of the north, thought anywhere south sounded like heaven.

At this season of the year darkness fell quickly in New York, and afternoon shadows were already stretching over the slushy streets by the time Mollie reached her new apartment. She still could not think of the place as home; she had lived in it only a few weeks.

When she had come to New York on her own, she had rented a single room. The new apartment was small by midwestern standards, but Mollie hardly had any furniture, and after the cramped confines of the one room, the apartment felt huge. The two and a half rooms seemed to echo like caverns, and tonight she knew the message that would throb through their emptiness: "Rent money? Rent? Rent?"

She unlocked the multiple locks on her door, entered the apartment and hung up her jacket, cap and muffler. She kicked off her boots and looked about at the bareness and gloom. The place might only be twice as big as her room had been, but it was more than five times as expensive.

Still, she and Michael had to live somewhere, and he had a considerable savings account for them to fall back on. She had managed to stretch her budget far enough to buy a used bed and a sofa that had seen happier days.

When Michael came, he would bring the furniture from his apartment in Minneapolis. She could hardly wait. The apartment now seemed cheerless and lonely.

Mollie curled up on the old sofa, hugging herself to force warmth back into her shivering body. Like many older apartments, this one had a fickle heating system and was often chilly. She shuddered and thought of the fate of poor Clarice. She shook her head sadly and listened to the emptiness of the apartment.

"Rent, rent, rent," the rooms seemed to whisper. "You just lost your job. What about the rent?"

She squared her shoulders. She could get back her part-time job as a waitress in Greene's Cafe. If she didn't find another acting job soon, she'd find full-time work of some kind, somewhere. She'd never been afraid of work. Nobody had ever told her that breaking into acting would be easy. Both she and Michael knew that, although she suspected it frightened Michael more than her. It shouldn't, she thought fondly, because Michael had talent, enormous talent.

She glanced at her watch. It wasn't yet five o'clock and she needed to stop feeling sorry for herself and do something. She must call her agent, Clytie Prokopoulos. She picked up the phone, which sat inelegantly on the floor, and dialed.

"Prokopoulos and Associates," Clytie answered in her abrupt voice. "Yes?"

"Clytie, it's Mollie Randall. They're killing my character on 'Doctors' Hospital.' I've only got another two weeks left."

Clytie, who was small, dark and passionate, swore. "I *hate* the writers on 'Doctors' Hospital!' Mass murderers are what they are. Everybody I get to work there they kill within six months. A curse should fall on them."

"Clytie, I'm desperate. This comes at the worst time."

"It always does, sweetie," Clytie said glumly. "Merry Christmas."

"Is anything opening up? Commercials, anything?"

"Darling, I'd let you know. Isn't that my job? I tell you everything I hear."

"Something steady," Mollie said, almost pleading. "If I could just get something steady, just for a while."

"You and a thousand other out-of-work actors," Clytie answered. "Wait. Let me look." Mollie heard the rustle of papers. "You're not so easy to cast, you know.

You and your freckles. And you've got so little professional experience.''

"Well, I can't get any more experience unless somebody *gives* it to me," Mollie argued. "And I've been on a national television show for the last six months. That should count for something—even if my character has been unconscious the whole time."

"Okay, okay, hang on," Clytie muttered. "Here. I got word there's going to be a casting call for an off-off-Broadway musical called *Bath House.* But you've got to take your clothes off for the part."

"I'm an actress," Mollie said with as much dignity as she could. "I will not stoop to showing my naked body."

"Okay, darling, okay." Clytie sighed. "I'm only asking. All right. Tomorrow you could try the Palmer Casting Agency. They're looking for a woman who can do an authentic Latvian accent."

"Latvian?" asked Mollie, dismayed. She wasn't even sure where Latvia was, let alone what its residents sounded like.

"Sweetie, I'm telling you what I've *got,*" Clytie said bluntly. "Okay, there's a casting call for a wholesome type to be in a commercial for the Burger House franchise. You could try for that. It wouldn't hurt. I also have word that one of the soaps needs a girl to play a junior high student... No, they'd never go for you, you're too tall and your voice is too low."

"Anything, Clytie. Anything. I'm getting married in two weeks. Somebody in the family needs a job."

"Two weeks," Clytie mumbled. "You don't need an agent, my dear girl, you need a miracle worker. Let's see. Right after the New Year, an educational company starts taping an audiovisual series on health. There's a couple of voice parts. It doesn't pay much."

"I don't care," Mollie said. "Just give me the name and address."

"Dear heart, I know you don't want to hear this, but you'd get a lot more work if you'd take your clothes off," Clytie said.

"I told you," Mollie said, "I won't do that. I'm not a showgirl. I'm an *actress.*"

"Not if you're not acting, you're not," Clytie said pointedly. "I'll tell you what you are, sweet child. You're young. You're a babe in the woods. This is not Minnesota. This is the big city, the mean streets. Sometimes you have to compromise."

Mollie lifted her chin. "Never."

"I mean it. Cupcake, not to insult you, but is this boyfriend of yours more realistic than you? You two are picking a *rough* way to make a living."

"I know, I know," Mollie said. " 'There's a broken heart for every light on Broadway,' and all that sort of stuff. But, Clytie, we're going to *make* it, Michael and I. We've dreamed of this for four years."

There was a moment of silence from Clytie's end of the line. "Sweetheart," Clytie said at last, "I hope this doesn't come as news. You can't eat dreams."

Mollie sat taller on the one ragged piece of furniture in the room. "We will if we have to," she said.

She meant it. Without dreams, she thought, a person might as well be dead.

MOLLIE SPENT THE NEXT DAY trudging from one casting director's office to another through streets wet with snow and thick with Christmas crowds.

She was tired, footsore, but relatively happy. She had not gotten the part that required the Latvian accent, and she was told her voice was too low for the girl in the Burger House commercial.

But heaven had at last smiled. The educational project on health had a part for her on the sound track of three videos. She would start immediately after the New Year. She would be the voice of a germ.

All right, she told herself as she crossed her lobby toward the mailboxes, the part wasn't exactly Lady Macbeth, but the pay would be almost enough for a month's rent. She wouldn't feel so terrible now about telling Michael that her part in the soap opera was cancelled. She had one decent job lined up and was determined to find others. She would walk the soles off her shoes if she had to.

She unlocked the mailbox, was momentarily dispirited by the number of bills, then felt a surge of cheer when she saw there was a thick envelope from Michael. She forgot about the bills, forgot about the imminent demise of Clarice, forgot about the indignity of being a germ. Grasping the stack of mail with happy possessiveness, she almost raced up the eight flights of stairs to her apartment.

She was breathless and her heart beat fast as she stepped inside the apartment and shrugged out of her coat. She tossed the rest of the mail onto one end of the couch, then curled into the opposite corner with Michael's letter. Her muffler was still draped around her neck, her fuzzy knit cap still pulled down over her red-blond hair.

She kicked off her boots and snuggled more deeply into the couch, wiggling her toes as she opened the letter. She smiled as she drew the four folded pages from the envelope.

She shook out the pages and began reading. Her smile faded. The blood drained from her face, making her freckles stand out. Her lips went pale.

"I can't go through with it," Michael wrote in his small, spiked handwriting. "I just can't marry you, Mollie. Although I'm fond of you, I've always had this feeling deep down that we weren't really right for each other. I've found somebody else..."

No, she thought. She felt as if the air around her was turning dark and smothering, as if all the light and oxygen were being sucked from the room. Unable to breathe, she felt a cramping heaviness in her chest, a nauseating knot in her stomach.

No, she thought again, sitting on the worn couch in the falling darkness. *This isn't possible.*

She read the opening paragraph again. Every word registered on her mind like a numbing blow.

Michael didn't want to marry her. He didn't love her. He'd found somebody else. She felt as if she were plunging down into a dark abyss, disappearing from ordinary life forever. Nothing would ever be the same again.

She read the rest of the letter in shock, only half comprehending.

Michael said that they were too different. Although Mollie had always thought that they could succeed as actors in New York, in his heart, Michael had never been able to believe it. It was a delusion. A struggling young actor's life was full of poverty and disappointment, and Michael had come to realize he wanted none of it.

He had gone along with Mollie's dreams, he said, because she was so persuasive and flattering, but when he thought about these matters soberly, he saw how impossible her plans were.

His doubts had kept him behind for a year in Minneapolis. He had said he wanted to earn another degree in case he had to fall back on teaching for a while. In truth, however, he had never really wanted to make the move to New York.

He had tried to believe in her dreams, he said, he really had. But the closer the wedding date drew, the more he knew that it wasn't going to work. And now he had found a woman, one more suited to him, another graduate student.

He and the woman were two of a kind, he said, artistic but practical. She wanted to teach, and so, he realized, did he. They wanted to live quiet but creative lives in a small college community somewhere.

Instead of coming to New York for Christmas, he would be going to meet the woman's parents in Corning, Iowa. He finished:

Mollie, you're an extraordinary person and have extraordinary talent. But even extraordinary people can't always make it. There's a song about dreaming the impossible dream. That's what I can't do. I can only dream the possible dream.

I know this will hurt you, and I hate that, but it's better that it happens now than later. It would never have worked between us, not really. I wish you all the best. But I can't take the path you've chosen. I hope life brings you wonderful luck. I'll always remember you with affection.

With regret,
Michael

P.S. I'm sorry you've already rented the apartment, but maybe you can sublet it or get a roommate. You can still return the plane tickets to New Orleans and get a full refund if you do it within the week. I checked for you.

Mollie stared at the letter in disbelief. She should have felt grief, but she was too stunned to feel anything. She and Michael had known each other for four years. They had met during their sophomore year in the drama department at college.

They began dating when she played the part of Maria to his Tony in the college's production of *West Side Story,* and until she had gone ahead to New York, she and Michael had been inseparable.

Their junior year, they had the leads in *The King and I.* During their senior year she had been Eliza Doolittle to his Henry Higgins in *My Fair Lady.* In between musicals they had worked together on half a dozen other projects, from one-act plays to Shakespeare. They existed for the stage; it had been their lives.

She had thought he was the most gifted young man she'd ever met, almost a genius. Both of them were besotted with the theater; they talked of nothing else.

Michael was not only talented, he was handsome. He was only slightly taller than Mollie, with a compact body, and so graceful that he moved as fluidly as a trained dancer. He was dark, with black hair and black eyes that could flash or brood with equal intensity.

She had thought they shared everything: affection, thoughts, hopes, plans. She had been wrong. Completely wrong.

Suddenly she became aware that although she was hurt, deeply hurt, she was also angry. She was extremely angry.

Why had he lied to her all this time about his dreams of coming to New York? Or had he been lying to himself, as well? If he'd had doubts, why hadn't he had the courage to voice them? If he had reservations, why hadn't he been honest enough to name them?

Besides that, how could he have been devious enough to be engaged to one woman in New York while he wooed another in Minneapolis? And with all his talent, he wanted to be a teacher? Michael was afraid of New York. Michael had been afraid of honesty. He was a coward.

She would phone him, she thought desperately, even though she couldn't afford it. Perhaps this was all some ghastly mistake, a terrible misunderstanding. But when she dialed Michael's number, all she got was a busy signal.

Michael, she thought in disgust, *I know what you're doing. You've got the phone unplugged. You always do it when you don't want to face something. You're afraid to talk to me.*

Her emotions began to career from one extreme to the other. Michael was her darling, her gifted soul mate, whom she had lost and would forever mourn. He was a lily-livered, lying wretch, devious and unmanly, and she was lucky to be rid of him. She would do anything, yes, anything, to have him back. No, she wouldn't take him back if he crawled on his hands and knees, dressed in sackcloth and with ashes in his hair.

Her emotions rocketed first one way, then another. Sometimes she cried. Sometimes she paced the almost empty room and kicked the sofa with impotent rage.

She stayed up all night, her emotions too stormy for sleep. In the end she decided two things. One was that although Michael had deceived her, she had also deceived herself about him. Hadn't she always sensed it in him—the fear, the reluctance to take a chance?

He had great talent, but talent alone wasn't enough. Instinctively she had always understood that. A person had to have dedication and determination and heart. A person had to be a fighter. But Michael was frightened of taking chances. He wasn't a fighter.

Mollie was. She came from a family where independence was prized and individuality expected. Her father, who was somewhat eccentric, had met Michael last Christmas and said, "Take him if you have to have him, Moll. But he'll never go the distance. He doesn't have fire in his belly."

Fire, she thought emptily. She went to the bedroom closet where she kept the shoe box that held all the letters Michael had sent her since she'd come to New York. She took them into the kitchen and turned on the burner of the ancient stove. One by one she carefully fed the letters to the flames, until only the last one was left, the one in which he said goodbye.

Still stunned, but dry-eyed now, she reread it once more. "Goodbye, Michael," she said, her voice husky.

She let the fire take the pages and turn them to ash. The first dim rays of morning light were falling through the window.

So she wasn't going to be married at Christmas, after all. Quite the opposite. She would be alone.

She returned to the couch and sat, curled in its corner, feeling curiously dull and used up. It would be nice, she thought, to go home, but there was, at present, no home to go to. Her father had taken a one-year teaching position at the university in Ibadan, Nigeria, and her mother had closed up the house in Minnesota and gone with him. Her brother was teaching English in Tokyo. Her sister was working with the Peace Corps in South America. This Christmas, Mollie didn't have an immediate relative on the entire continent of North America.

She thought once again of her father, and of the advice he'd given all of his children. "Rule Number One," he'd told them, "don't think of yourself as a victim or you'll be one. Self-pity is the most debilitating emotion in the world."

All right, she thought, nodding in silent affirmation. She wouldn't be a victim. She refused to feel helpless and she refused to be sorry for herself. It had never been the family's style, and it had never been hers. She lifted her chin stubbornly.

Her father had also used to say, with a slightly malicious twinkle in his eye, "When somebody hurts you, Moll, don't hurt them back. Do something nice instead—for yourself. Get even that way: living well is the best revenge."

She shrugged to herself. She had no desire to hurt Michael, not really. But there was nothing she could do to make herself feel better, not one thing.

Or was there?

She bit her lip, remembering the airline tickets in the kitchen drawer. She had lost her job and her fiancé. Her family was scattered over three foreign countries and she would be alone for the holidays. She was renting an apartment she couldn't afford and she had hardly any furniture. Her future held nothing loftier to look forward to than a job as the voice of a cold germ.

But she wasn't beaten, and she wouldn't say no to the joys that life still had to offer. Michael said she could turn in the plane tickets and get a refund. She would do so—with his.

She had planned one extravagance for Christmas, and she would have it. Michael might be visiting potential in-laws in Corning, Iowa. Mollie would go to New Orleans, the city Michael and she had dreamed about. What's more, she would have a marvelous time.

She went to the window and stared out at the brick wall that was her view. It was bathed in the thin light of the new winter morning. Snow had fallen all night long and was softly heaped upon the building's ledges. Veils of it lifted and drifted like ghosts in the wind.

She thought of New Orleans, where there was sunshine even in December. Flowers were blooming in New Orleans, palms trees tossed their fronds in the sun, the sky was blue, the air was warm and there was music in the streets.

She would go on her honeymoon, unmarried, alone—and free.

CHAPTER TWO

"IF YOU THINK YOU'VE got troubles, look around," Mollie's father always said. "Somebody always has more problems than you. Get interested. Nothing does you more good than lending a helping hand."

The first person Mollie noticed when she got on the crowded plane was the man sitting in the front row in the aisle seat. A jab of sympathy struck her heart. The man was tall, tanned and handsome. But he obviously had more problems than she did. He was blind.

Dark glasses hid his eyes and a guide dog lay at his feet. The dog, a German shepherd, was old and heavy, its muzzle growing gray. It lay with its head up, watching the other passengers carefully, and its amber eyes seemed almost human.

The man, in spite of his handicap, otherwise radiated health and power. His gray slacks hugged muscular thighs, and the heavy knit of his spruce-green sweater made his broad shoulders seem broader still. Beneath the sweater, he wore a white shirt, and the snowiness of its open collar emphasized the bronze of his skin.

Mollie knew intuitively he was not a native New Yorker, a creature of crowds and winter cold. He was a man unused to dull and wintry skies, sunless days or confined spaces.

His thick brown hair was swept straight back so that she could see his widow's peak. His jaw was square, his cheekbones pronounced and his nose aquiline.

It was his mouth that Mollie found most unusual, however. Well-cut, it conveyed a contradictory mix of impressions. It was sensitive yet cynical, controlled yet sensual. He sat straight, the dark glasses trained on the empty wall in front of him, as if he were lost in thought.

She examined her ticket again and felt a frisson of un-expected, unnameable emotion. The blind man was her seatmate. He was sitting where Michael was supposed to have sat on this trip.

Don't think of that, she told herself sternly. Instead she forced herself to remember her father's advice. She vowed that she would be as tactfully helpful to the man as she could. It must be perfectly hellish to be blind and traveling alone in the holiday rush.

She stowed her trench coat in the overhead storage space, then carefully stepped over the guide dog. She settled in the narrow seat beside the man. Once more she was struck by how he seemed to radiate an air of surpris-ing physical power.

"A beautiful dog," she said, to let the man know she was there and to establish if he wanted to talk.

He turned to face her, his expression solemn. "You flatter him. He's old. He's fat. And he creates the most extraordinary smells. An olfactory marvel."

Mollie stared at his solemn face in surprise, not know-ing what to reply. Then she saw dimples quiver in his tanned cheeks, and she smiled. She hadn't expected him to joke. Neither had she expected him to have an accent, but he did, a lazy southwestern drawl that was like honey laced with whiskey.

"How old is he?" she asked.

"In human years?" he asked in his slow voice. "Thirteen. In dog years, that makes him about ninety. He totters toward cootdom, but he does it with style. His name is Fritz. Mine's Pearce Goddard. Might we have the pleasure of yours?"

He extended his hand and she shook it. It was hard and strong, and pulsed with energy against her own. "Mollie. Mollie Randall."

He caressed her knuckles with deft fingers. "You have skin like new satin, Mollie Randall. Delicate. Do you freckle, by any chance?"

Mollie looked at him in astonishment. His black lenses reflected small images of her in their depths.

"As a matter of fact—I do," she said. Her freckles were a trial to her; she never lost them, not even in winter. She had even, in recent dark moments of the soul, wondered if Michael hadn't loved her because she was forever blemished by freckles. "You can tell that just by—by touching me?"

"A lucky guess. I have a highly developed sense of touch," he said, stroking the palm of her hand. "Hearing, too. Do you want me to tell you about yourself?"

Mollie nodded, then realized he couldn't see the motion. "Yes," she said, fascinated, letting her hand lie in his. "What can you tell?"

"Let me see—if you'll excuse the expression." He squeezed her hand. "You're slim from the feel of your bone structure. You're tall. I can tell that from the height your voice comes from. From the way you talk you're from the middle west; you pronounce all your *r*'s and don't distort your vowels. Either that or you've studied speech. Or maybe both."

"That's—amazing," Mollie said. She wished his touch didn't send tickles dancing up and down her spine. She was, after all, in mourning.

"But your voice," he said thoughtfully, shaking his head. "Your voice raises as many questions as it answers. It's velvety. But it's got a cute little froggy croak to it, too. An ageless voice. I can't get a fix on how old you are."

"Twenty-three," said Mollie, a bit awed.

"Twenty-three." He gave an appreciative nod, as if to himself. "Imagine that. Only twenty-three." He squeezed her hand more intimately.

He made her sound ridiculously young. He himself must be in his early thirties. Time had just begun to deepen the lines that bracketed his mouth, and the dark glasses did not completely hide the laugh lines that radiated from the corners of his eyes.

His fingers moved to her garnet ring, toying with it. "And this, I take it, is no engagement ring. It's on the wrong hand."

"There's no engagement ring," Mollie murmured. With a pang she thought once more of Michael. For once she didn't try to keep her face impassively blank. There was that to be said for talking with a blind man, she thought: she didn't have to will her face to turn to stone as she had done so often lately. She could let her emotions show without fearing anyone's pity.

At the same time, she was confused and embarrassed by the boldness of Pearce Goddard's touch. She realized that although he might be blind, he also had the potential to be a world-class womanizer. Perhaps his blindness somehow made him even more fascinating to the opposite sex. He'd said he had a highly developed sense of touch, and heaven knew, his touch against her hand was as sensual as could be imagined.

All Mollie was certain of was that she was in no mood for a flirtation, even one as brief as their short flight would allow. Her emotions were still too bruised, too vulnerable. She would not toy with them, nor would she allow anyone else to.

He had begun to caress her knuckles and palm again, slowly, as if savoring the feel of her. "Um," she said uncomfortably, wriggling slightly in her seat. "Do you—need my hand any more?"

He looked slightly startled, genuinely so, as if he'd forgotten he even had it. "Sorry," he said, but the slant of his mouth didn't look sorry.

Mollie distracted herself by trying to fasten her seat belt. A sign had flashed on, instructing passengers to do so. Mollie, who had never flown before, found it surprisingly difficult to master, but at last the two halves clicked together. On a teacher's salary, her father had never been able to afford to fly the family anywhere. They had taken their trips by car or not at all. Mollie had come to New York on a Greyhound bus. She was unnerved to find the prospect of flying intimidated her a bit, for she was not used to being intimidated.

"Did the seat belt sign come on?" Pearce asked. She saw one of his eyebrows arch up questioningly above the dark glasses.

"Yes," she said, then paused, regarding him uneasily. "Do you . . . can I help?"

"If you'd be so kind." He shrugged disarmingly, and the complicated line of his mouth seemed to smile. "These things work differently on every airline. To tell the truth, I haven't traveled alone that much. I'd ask the flight attendant, but it makes me feel—you know—conspicuous.''

Mollie bit her lip. Of course, she sensed, he would be a proud man, unwilling to trouble the attendant for assistance. But fastening his seat belt seemed an oddly intimate gesture.

''I'll be glad to help any way I can,'' she said gamely. ''Just let me know how.''

She had to bend across his lean body and grope against his hip to find the other half of the seat belt. Once again she found that the belt was surprisingly difficult to clamp into place. She was all too aware that her fingers were fumbling helplessly in a strange man's lap and that she had to maneuver herself disturbingly close to him to manipulate the buckle.

The dog raised its head and regarded her soberly, as if it suspected she had designs upon its master.

''What's your destination?'' Pearce asked, his drawling voice soft in her ear, making it burn.

''New Orleans,'' she said, profoundly relieved when the halves of the buckle clamped together. She settled back into her own seat, her fingers tingling oddly.

''What a coincidence,'' he said. ''Say, would you mind tightening this? It seems loose.''

''Not at all,'' Mollie lied, and clenched her teeth as she once more half leaned against him and tried to tighten the recalcitrant belt. Her shoulder kept brushing the sweatered hardness of his chest and she could smell his aftershave, which was like pine boughs and woodsmoke.

''I'm going to New Orleans myself.'' Once more his voice tickled her ear, made a stray tendril of her hair flutter.

''Oh,'' Mollie said with false brightness as the belt refused to budge. ''Do you have family there?''

"No." His breath fanned her cheek, and she grew more conscious of the warm and piny scent that clung about him. "I'm meeting—a friend."

The way he said "friend" made her suspect the friend was a woman. She wouldn't be surprised a bit, and yet, she told herself, she shouldn't criticise. Given his handicap, it was admirable, perhaps even gallant, for him to have the spirit for flirtation.

"Are you connecting with flight 808 in Dallas?" he asked. "Ah—I think you've almost got it. You're very dexterous. Interesting."

Mollie gave a sigh of gratification as the belt finally tightened across his flat stomach. Once more she settled back in her seat. Why did it make her so uneasy to touch him, even accidentally? Because she had touched no man except Michael for so long? She tried to clear her head, to remember Pearce's question and answer it.

"Flight 808?" she said vaguely. "Yes. Is that yours, too?"

He nodded. "It'll be nice to have a friendly person heading in the same direction. It gives me—confidence. You seem like a kind child." He folded his hands together and nodded again, as if in satisfaction. "A very kind child."

Mollie was tempted to reply that she was hardly a child, and to point out that the last thing he seemed to require was more confidence, but she only raised her eyebrow. She remembered her father's admonition to think of others' troubles, not her own. "I'll be glad to do anything I can."

Pearce settled back more comfortably, his lips pursing thoughtfully. "I can imagine any number of wonderful things you might do for me."

He smiled slightly, as if contemplating them. Once more the black glasses looked directly at the blank wall before them.

Mollie said nothing. Suddenly she seemed exhausted by the emotions that she had struggled so hard to control for the past weeks. Her nerves were also on edge at the prospect of flying, for it was beginning to occur to her that flying was both an unnatural act and a risky one.

The jet, with every seat filled, seemed overloaded, far too heavy to take off safely. Outside, through the twilight air, snowflakes were starting to drift down. Would a snowstorm engulf them? She swallowed.

A flight attendant came to the front of the cabin, stood in the center of the aisle and made a depressing speech about what to do in case of disaster: she recited a frightening litany about flotation devices, oxygen masks and emergency exits. Mollie listened and swallowed again.

Then the jet's engines thrummed into life, vibrating so hard that she felt their resonations deep in her spine. Slowly the craft began to taxi up the runway, at first at a lumbering pace, then with increasing speed as the noise of the takeoff roared more loudly.

She gripped the arms of her seat as hard as she could. The plane gave one stomach-wrenching bump, then another, and finally lifted uneasily from the ground, like a ponderous but determined bird.

Pearce's hand settled on hers by apparent accident. He drew it away immediately. "Excuse me," he said, but then he laid his hand atop hers again. "Good Lord, you're tense," he said. "Haven't you flown before?"

Mollie, her shoulders tautened uncomfortably, shook her head. She realized he couldn't see the gesture, and it was probably just as well he couldn't see how obviously nervous she must look. She made her voice sound calmer than she felt. "Never," she said lightly. "But just give me a minute. I'll get used to it."

He gave her hand a pat that was almost brotherly, then laced his fingers together in his lap. "Ask for a magazine. Or rent earphones and watch the movie. Read a book if you brought one. You'll forget you're even in the air."

"Thanks," Mollie said, for his advice seemed both kindly and sound. She paused. What about him? she wondered. She might distract herself with a book, magazine or movie, but what would he do? He was disturbingly flirtatious, but should she talk to him during the flight? He would spend the three hours marooned in darkness.

"What about you?" she asked. "Can I do anything? I hate to let you just—sit."

He smiled to himself as he crossed one leg over the other. "You watch your movie. I'll watch mine. I show it on the back of my eyelids. I make it up. Do you ever do that?"

Mollie stared at him with fresh bewilderment. He was, she thought, such an unexpected man, full of surprises. She had never met anyone like him. "You make up a movie?" she asked. "About what? About anything you want?"

He leaned his head back against the seat, his black glasses trained on nothing in particular. "No. It's always the same movie. About a mole."

"A mole?" Mollie asked, hardly noticing that the plane shook slightly as it banked away from the airport. "You mean a mole in the spy sense—like a person who tunnels into an enemy organization?"

He shook his head lazily. "No. A mole in the small, insectivorous mammal sense. An animal."

She smiled in amused perplexity. "But why? Why a mole?" What could the man possibly imagine?

"Because I *love* this mole movie," he said with satisfaction. "Ah. The credits are starting. The theme music's rising." His smile grew more cryptic. He seemed pleased to grow lost in a world of his own making.

The dog looked at him, shook its head twice, sighed and settled its grizzled muzzle on its paws. It closed its amber eyes warily and almost immediately began to snore. It snored loudly, and from time to time, strange gurgling noises issued from the depths of its stomach.

The plane gave a rather unnerving dip, but Mollie told herself to be calm: flying was an adventure, and she should be glad, not apprehensive. She was on her way to New Orleans at last, just as she had planned.

No, she thought with a surge of bitterness that she struggled to fight down. Things weren't exactly as she'd planned.

She was supposed to have been married on this day. Instead, her fiancé was probably already somewhere in Iowa, meeting the parents of the woman he intended to marry instead of Mollie.

She was supposed to have made this trip sitting next to her new husband. Instead she was making it with a fat, snoring, gurgling German shepherd lying at her feet. At her side was not serious, practical Michael, but a flirtatious blind man, lost in his own peculiar thoughts, happily making up a movie about a mole.

"Mollie," her father had always said, "life hardly ever goes the way you expect. Don't try to figure it out. Just sit back and enjoy its oddity. Because that's what gives it its greatest charm. It's very, very odd."

All right, Mollie thought philosophically and squared her shoulders. *I'll learn to appreciate oddity.*

She opened the book she had brought, a fat novel of glitter and romance. But when, in the first chapter, the heroine's husband committed adultery and left her for another woman, Mollie could bear to read no further. Once more thoughts of Michael came unbidden, this time so strongly that her eyes smarted with tears. Angrily she scrubbed them away, glad that the man beside her could not see her shame.

She closed her eyes in weariness. She slept.

A GARBLED ANNOUNCEMENT crackling over the plane's PA system woke Mollie. She was confused and startled to discover she was nestled warmly against Pearce Goddard, her head resting on the solidness of his shoulder.

She drew away, embarrassed. She was not usually the type who nuzzled up to men or leaned on them. She moved so swiftly that she disturbed Fritz, the dog, who stared up at her with wounded dignity.

"Umm," she said, stretching and trying to sound cool. "I'm sorry. I didn't mean—"

"I didn't mind," he said, unsmiling. "Did you hear what the pilot said? We've got trouble."

"Trouble?" She blanched. Visions of accidents flamed in her head. She tried to remember what the flight attendant had said about flotation devices, oxygen masks, emergency exits. Once more she gripped the arms of her seat. "Are we going to crash?"

His mouth took on one of its unreadable quirks. "No. That would be dramatic, but simple. Over fast. We've got dull trouble. Complicated and dragged out. The planes are backed up over Dallas. We're going to be at least an hour late. Bad weather. More on the way."

Mollie relaxed, momentarily relieved. Then she frowned. "But we were late when we boarded. If we're another hour late..."

He nodded grimly. "Right. We miss our connection. Unless it's delayed, too."

Mollie groaned. She didn't need to have anything go wrong with this trip. Enough had already gone awry in her life. She put her hand to her forehead and wondered, pessimistically, if she had developed some sort of reverse Midas touch. Everything she touched lately seemed to turn to trouble and disappointment.

Pearce grimaced slightly. "The pilot said this weather's affecting most of the south. We may face a nasty case of airport roulette once we land. Who knows when we'll get out?"

"When we'll get out?" Mollie asked in horror. "You mean we could be there all *night?*"

"My dear," he said from between his teeth, "we might be lucky if we're only there all night. If things are bad enough, we could get stuck there for *days.*"

"Days?" She didn't bother to keep the dismay from her voice.

"It happens," he said with an impatient shrug. "And it's going to be confusing. You've never done this before?"

"Never."

"All right," he said. "Then stick with me. We're trying to get to the same place. We can help each other out. Okay?"

"Of course," she agreed gratefully. He might be flirtatious, but he was also courtly in his flippant way. She had imagined herself taking care of him. He was proving more than capable of returning the favor.

"Now," he said, "do just one favor for me, will you?"

"I'll be glad to do anything," she said, "anything at all."

He shook his head and smiled ruefully. "Miss Randall, a girl with a voice like yours should never, ever tell a man she'll do anything. His heart might stop with happiness."

"I didn't mean it that way," she said, slightly shaken. He really was a most disconcerting man, she thought; he was impossible, in fact.

"More's the pity," he said with a false sigh. "No, all I ask is that you signal the flight attendant, wherever she is. I need a cup of coffee. I usually don't try to eat or drink on a plane—too much hassle. But if I'm going into battle, I could use some caffeine for fortification."

"I'll be glad to," she said.

"And help me make sure that I don't spill coffee on the dog, will you? It always puts him in a rotten mood."

Mollie ordered the coffee, and because the weather over Texas had grown turbulent, she helped Pearce drink it. Her fingers could not keep from touching his strong, tanned ones, and once her knuckle accidently brushed the warm curve of his lip.

They spilled coffee on the dog only once. At the affront, he looked up at them accusingly, as if he were the only one of the threesome who had the sense to be serious.

DALLAS WAS A MAJOR HUB for air travel in the United States, and when it experienced trouble, it sent out shock waves that shuddered across the country's entire air system.

The terminal was nightmarish, for it was experiencing a double crisis. Not only were most flights, both incoming and outgoing, delayed by the bad weather, it was crammed with teeming hoards of holiday travelers, all anxious to be at a thousand destinations other than Dallas.

Nor was Dallas the only airport experiencing a weather catastrophe. Mollie and Pearce soon learned that a series of storms was assaulting most of the south. Atlanta, another major hub of service, was shut down completely. So were Memphis, Miami, Tampa, Mobile and Houston. It was snowing in Orlando, frosting in San Antonio, and even New Orleans—sunny, semitropical New Orleans—was swept by cold and ice, freezing its airport into partial paralysis.

While Pearce tried to extract information from a beleaguered airline clerk, Mollie looked about her in consternation. The picture reminded her of a scene in a war movie, with thousands of desperate people trying in vain to escape some besieged place.

She saw almost every sort of person: male, female, young, old, rich and not rich, and an assortment of nationalities. She saw almost every sort of expression written on their faces. Some were angry and some were confused; some were frustrated and rigid with tension, some resigned and weary. A few were calm, a few managed to smile and a few were wild-eyed, looking ready to break under the strain.

I have to remember this, Mollie told herself. All these faces, all these emotions; as an actress she should store them in her memory. She had never before seen so many different emotions churning through a crowd. But the thought was small comfort in the airport's crush.

People were everywhere. They filled every seat, leaned against every available section of wall space; some even lay on the floor, their coats beneath their heads, trying to snatch a few moments of sleep in the midst of all the pandemonium.

Pearce turned from the ticket agent's desk. She took a step nearer to him, putting her hand on his arm. He wore a light jacket with a flannel lining, and she had put on her trench coat. "What's the story?" she asked.

With one arm he drew her nearer. With his other hand he clamped the handle of Fritz's harness more tightly. "Stay close to me. They've changed the departure gate. We're at number 2 now. We've got to get to 36—that'll be a way off. We'll have to hurry and we have a crowd to fight."

She gripped his arm more tightly, looking up at him. He was even taller than she had thought, six foot three at least. Her heart was beating fast, fluttering in her chest, but he seemed calm, sure of himself. Fritz, his eyes on his master, seemed oblivious to the confusion swarming around them.

"Fritz understands directional commands—right, left, forward. Tell me how to get to gate 36 and he'll get us there."

She searched the profusion of signs suspended from the ceiling. "Forward," she said.

"Forward," Pearce repeated. "Hang on."

They began weaving through the crowd with a speed and precision that amazed her.

It took only a few moments for Mollie's respect for the dog to heighten into something approaching awe. Fritz saw openings that a human would have missed, quickly spotted obstacles a human might not have seen until too late.

Ears up, Fritz plunged and weaved through the sea of humanity without error and at a pace that was truly startling. He dodged, he zigged, he zagged, but he always kept moving forward. No wonder Pearce Goddard was in such excellent shape, she thought, struggling to hang on to him; keeping up with the dog demanded muscle and speed.

"Ouff!" she cried as she crashed into a fat man loaded with Christmas presents. She apologized as best she could and took tighter hold of Pearce's arm.

"Stay a little bit behind me," Pearce warned. "Fritz isn't used to calculating for more than one person behind him."

She was starting to feel breathless. She spotted another sign for gate 36, its arrow pointing in a new direction. "Left!" she said, and when Pearce repeated the command, she veered to keep up with him.

"Good grief," she almost panted, "you're so *fast*. Is this why more people don't have guide dogs?"

He grinned down at her. He had a white, wide grin, full of irreverence. "You should have known him when he was young. He almost flew. He could get you across Times Square at midnight on New Year's Eve if he had to. And you're right, not everybody can keep up with a dog. Some people think they're too much trouble, or they don't like them or trust them. Me, I think these dogs should get a special place in heaven. And it should be the one with the best view."

The thought was a fanciful one, but she liked it. Dogs that had spent their lives seeing for others should spend eternity seeing what they themselves most liked. She smiled up at him. "What's the best view from dog heaven?"

He shrugged. "Maybe cat heaven. Who knows? If we get to heaven, we'll have to ask."

Fritz dodged two children racing in and out of the crowd and a man struggling with three boxes marked

Caution! Live Lobsters! Mollie had to sidestep quickly to avoid the man with the lobsters, and she almost lost hold of Pearce's arm again.

"Left again," she cried, spying a new sign.

She was out of breath, her legs weak and her mouth dry by the time they reached the gate. "We're here," she said gratefully. "The ticket line is straight ahead. But oh, Pearce, it's really crowded and everyone looks unhappy—grouchy, depressed and restless. There's no place to sit here, either."

She paused, looking up at the banks of screens with their televised lists of arrival and departure times. "Oh, no," she said, shaking her head in consternation. "The flight's been delayed. After all that hurry—and they don't even hint when it might take off. *Drat.*"

He seemed unfazed. "Give me your ticket," he ordered as they took their place in line.

"What?" she asked. "Why?"

"Let me take care of this," he said firmly. "It'll be easier to do two at once. Besides, I've done this kind of thing before, and you haven't."

"But," she said, "I can do it for myself. You already stood in line at the first place—"

He reached out, rather tentatively, until he found her. Then his touch became sure and firm as he clasped her upper arm. "We're partners during this trip, right? You and Fritz help me see. I'll do my part and take care of the accommodations. If you want to do me a favor, scout this place for a bar. If I ever hear that we're going to make it out of here, I want to celebrate with a beer."

"It's a deal," she said. "Only I'll buy."

"We'll argue about that *if* you find beer," he said, lifting a cynical brow, "and I find a flight." He squeezed her arm, then released it and turned his attention toward the counter, his eyes masked by the dark glasses.

She looked at him, then at Fritz. The old dog had not flagged once during its long trip to the gate, but now it looked exhausted. It was panting and breathing hard, its head down and ribs heaving. She thought she could perceive the finest of tremors shaking its sturdy legs.

Her heart wrenched. "Is he all right?" she asked huskily. "Fritz, I mean. He looks all worn out."

Pearce didn't turn his face toward her. His expression showed no emotion, and the set of his mouth was abnormally straight. "He's a soldier. He'll be fine."

She stared again at Fritz. His eyes were half-closed with weariness, his tongue lolling from his gray muzzle.

The dog was so old, she thought. How long had Fritz and Pearce been companions? Years, she supposed, ever since the dog was young and newly trained. How terrible for such a loyal and trusted animal to grow old, to lose its strength. How would Pearce feel when the dog was no longer able to work? What happened to old guide dogs, anyway? She had no idea what became of them once they had passed their prime. And how hard would it be for Pearce to adjust to a new dog after all these years with Fritz?

"Are you still here?" Pearce asked impatiently. "You're supposed to be the scout in this outfit. Beer, woman. In the name of all that's holy. Or unholy, as the case may be."

"I'll do my best," she said, and slipped through the crowd, leaving him with the exhausted dog at his side.

Fortunately, there was a small cocktail lounge not far from the gate, although every seat was taken and many patrons were standing. She wondered if she and Pearce would even be able to make their way to the bar.

Turning, she struggled through the swarm of humanity to get back to their gate. She couldn't find a seat, but she did find a pillar to lean against, and she did so gratefully. She could see Pearce from her vantage point, his head slightly above the rest of the crowd, his dark glasses hiding his eyes. From a distance, his expression looked serious, almost relentless.

She leaned her head back against the pillar, closed her eyes and sighed. She allowed herself to make a soft, short sound that resembled a bitter laugh deep in her throat. Today was to have been her wedding day, tonight her wedding night.

But instead of honeymooning with her husband in a hotel in New Orleans, she was probably going to be stranded in the Dallas airport. Her only companions were a blind man about whom she knew nearly nothing and an elderly dog about which she was worried.

Once again she felt all the tumultuous emotions she had held in for the last few weeks growing unruly, wanting to break free and run away with her. She bit her lip and forced herself to open her eyes. Michael wasn't here beside her. He would never be beside her again. That was that.

She kept her eyes fixed on Pearce Goddard, his lean face, his thick brown hair with its widow's peak. She was probably better off in this emergency with the blind man, she told herself with brutal irony. He, at least, knew what he was doing.

Michael was like her. He'd never been far from home and had never been on a jet in his life. He would have loathed coping with all this chaos. He hated delays, he hated confusion, and strange places and situations often filled him with such uneasiness that he tended to sulk or snap. He was never pleasant when he was nervous, and this snag in their trip would have made him as nervous as he was on an opening night, when he was always impossible....

I won't think about him, she told herself fiercely. *I won't think anything about him, good or bad.* She would think instead about getting Pearce Goddard safely to New Orleans and she would worry about his tired and aging dog. She had far too much to deal with to be thinking of Michael.

She was relieved to see Pearce talking earnestly with one of the clerks, apparently being extremely insistent about something. At last he seemed satisfied and stepped away from the desk, then stood, waiting. She knew he was waiting for her.

Hurriedly she made her way to him and laid her hand upon his arm. Even through his jacket she could feel the hardness of his muscles.

"Will the plane take off? Did you get our seats confirmed?"

"Yes and yes," he said. "Now for the important question. Did you find a place to get a beer?"

"Straight ahead, about fifty yards," she said, "but it's crowded. When can we get out of here?"

He gave Fritz the command to go forward, and once more Mollie found herself clinging to Pearce's arm as he and the dog made swift and unerring progress through the crowd.

"New Orleans is covered with ice. Their airport isn't prepared to deal with it. But they're going to try two flights in. One in half an hour, another in an hour and a half. We leave in an hour and a half. I had to wrangle to keep us together. They wanted to send me ahead. Because of this." He tapped the rim of his dark glasses contemptuously.

"But you should have gone," she said, squeezing closer to him so they wouldn't be separated. "You have your friend waiting for you."

"My friend," he said, his mouth sardonic, "was supposed to fly out of Tampa. Nothing's flying out of Tampa and nothing's likely to. They're getting the worst of this. No. Nobody's waiting for me. So... I could use your help. All right?"

He put his free hand over hers and gave it a friendly squeeze. Warmth surged through her. "Of course," she said, glad he trusted her. "I'm depending on you as much as you are on me. But how did you manage to keep us together?"

"Easy," he said with an irreverent grin. "I told them this was our honeymoon. And I wasn't going on it without you."

His words pierced her heart. The warmth that had been tingling through her vanished. She felt numbed, stunned. "What?" she demanded. She stopped in her tracks.

He stopped, too. "What's the problem?" he said, frowning. "Is the idea that disgusting?" The dog stared at them both over its shoulder, puzzlement in its eyes.

She found she was almost trembling in agitation. "It's a *lie*," she managed to say. Worse, she thought, shaken, it was a lie about what she had just been trying so hard to forget: her honeymoon.

"It's a small white lie," he said from between clenched teeth. "For our mutual good. It's no big deal. All's fair in love, war and airline delays."

No, Mollie thought, looking up at his dark glasses and the cynical expression of his mouth. *All's not fair in love.* She thought of Michael and how his thousands of tiny untruths had turned into major deception.

"I hate lies," she said, struggling to keep her voice even. She was glad Pearce couldn't see her face. She knew she looked distraught, but for once she couldn't help it. His remark had brought all her stifled emotions surging dangerously to the surface. "I hate all lies. Big ones, small ones, black ones, white ones. I don't care how good a cause they're for."

"What's done is done," he said, his voice brusque. A frown creased his brow. "Take it easy, will you? Where's the bar? You sound like you could use a drink yourself."

"To the left," she said with resignation. She shouldn't have reacted so violently. How could he know the word *honeymoon* stabbed through her like a knife? How could he know about Michael's betrayal?

She squeezed closer to him again by way of mute apology. He probably thought she found the idea of marriage to a blind man repellent, but that was not true. Pearce Goddard was an extremely attractive man, tall, powerful, handsome, quick of wit and carrying himself with more confidence than most sighted men.

"I'm sorry," she said softly. "I guess I'm just keyed up from all the confusion."

"It's all right," he said. His tone was gruff, but he put his hand over hers where it rested on his arm and squeezed it.

They tried to move into the bar, but it was so crowded that even Fritz was momentarily stymied. The three of them stopped, wedged among the throng of patrons.

Mollie was surprised to feel a hand on her shoulder and hear a heavily accented voice in her ear. "Here, lady. Take our seats. We've been in here three hours. Long enough."

She whirled. She and Pearce were crowded almost against the bar itself, and two Japanese businessmen were rising from their bar stools. It was one of the two men who had touched her and spoken to her.

He smiled and nodded toward their seats. "Merry Christmas," he said.

"Oh," Mollie said with gratitude, "bless you! I mean it."

The men held the seats for them until Mollie guided Pearce to one stool and took the other for herself. "Good grief," she said. "Seats. That almost qualifies as a Christmas miracle."

Fritz made a sound between a sigh and a groan and settled down at Pearce's feet, curling himself up as tightly as possible. He looked about wearily, as if certain he was going to be stepped on. Mollie planted her feet firmly on his other side to give him a bit more protection.

"I hope that was for your sake, not mine," Pearce said, nodding in her direction. His mobile mouth had taken on a moody cast. "I don't want any special treatment."

"Nonsense," Mollie said. "We'll have a beer and then give the seats to somebody else. I'll watch for somebody who looks deserving."

"What'll it be?" asked a round-faced bartender who looked harried and out of patience.

"Do you like German beer? Dark?" Pearce asked Mollie.

"I love it," she said.

"Two beers," Pearce said. "Make them German and make them dark. I'm paying."

Mollie dug into her purse and pulled out her billfold. "No, you're not," she said, taking out a five-dollar bill.

But he had already drawn out his wallet and extracted a couple of bills. They were folded, she noticed, and supposed the folds were made so that he could tell one denomination from another.

"We're out of imports. We got American beer left, period. No glasses. No napkins. No peanuts. No snacks."

"Two *American* beers, then," Pearce said in disgust. "And take my money. If the lady pays, forget your tip. I'll have the dog eat it."

Cheerlessly the bartender looked first at Pearce's money, then at Mollie's. He took Pearce's, reached under the bar, unceremoniously set two bottles before them, opened them, then lumbered away. Mollie put her billfold back in her purse and set the heavy bag beside her on the floor, close to her feet.

"Here," she said, and moved the beer bottle near Pearce's hand so he could find it without groping.

"Thanks," he said and took a long drink. "Ah. Ambrosia." He didn't turn his face toward her. He kept his dark glasses trained on some spot beyond the bar. Several emotions seemed to play across his lips, and Mollie wondered how it was possible for a human mouth to express so much and so little at the same time.

"So," he said, his voice light and slightly bored. "What's taking you to New Orleans? Friends? Family?"

"Neither," she answered, looking down at her hands clasped on the bar. "I don't know anybody."

He raised an eyebrow dubiously. "You're staying for the holidays?"

She nodded, forgetting once more that he couldn't see her. "For Christmas, yes." She tried to keep her tone as light and careless as his.

"*Alone* for Christmas?" he asked, turning to face her.

"Yes," she said with a shrug.

"Why?" he demanded. "You don't seem like the type."

She kept gazing at her clenched hands. She didn't want to look at his face. How could she tell such a handsome man she'd just been jilted? What would he think of her? She would be humiliated.

"It seemed like a good idea at the time," she said, struggling to keep her voice jaunty.

He took another sip of beer. He tilted his head slightly, which gave him a thoughtful air. "No family?"

"They're all out of the country."

He nodded, raising his eyebrow again. "No boyfriend?"

"Not at present," she said with artificial cheerfulness. "You know, I really don't feel like a beer, after all. You can have mine." She pushed her bottle next to his so that it grazed his knuckles. "And I'll leave the tip," she said. "I insist. Why don't you tell me about your mole movie. I'm curious . . . really."

She reached for her purse to get the money for the tip. She couldn't find it. She groped for it again, then stared at the floor where it should have rested.

It was gone. She stared with horror at the space that it had occupied.

Blood drained from her face. She felt stunned and giddy with fright. "Oh, no," she breathed, her throat choked. "My purse. It's been stolen."

"What?" he demanded.

Her heart began to knock in her chest. "It's been stolen," she repeated numbly. "It's gone."

"You didn't have hold of it?"

"No," she said, dazed, "but it was right here, beside me . . ."

He slapped the bar in disgust. "This place has got to be pickpocket paradise tonight. How much money did you have? I hope it was in traveler's checks."

She felt naive and stupid. "No," she said, shaking her head. "It was cash. Three hundred dollars. What'll I do?"

He threw another bill on the bar, then reached over and unerringly took her arm. "Come on," he said. "We'll contact airport security. Come on, Fritz. How do we get out of here?"

"Right," she said, and he echoed the word briskly.

She laced her arm through his numbly. "Maybe somebody picked it up by accident," she said. She felt more than slightly sick. It was as if someone had hollowed her out, then filled her with churning loss and a sense of violation.

"It was no accident," he said grimly, holding her arm and keeping her tightly at his side. "And they'll probably find your purse—eventually. But not with the money. If the thief was smart, he—or she—will leave your credit cards and checks. It's a lot safer and simpler to steal just cash. Nobody can trace it, and stealing cards can land you in federal prison."

"How can somebody steal at *Christmas?*" Mollie asked, a hard knot choking her throat. "How *could* they?"

"Honesty's in short supply all year round," he said cynically.

Honesty, thought Mollie darkly. It seemed to be going out of style.

PEARCE GAVE HER ARM an encouraging squeeze and pulled her nearer to him still. He set his mouth in a line as unreadable as possible.

He had sensed the woman was troubled from the time she'd sat down beside him on the plane. He was a perceptive man and he thought he could guess why she was troubled. It had to do with a man, and whoever the man was, he had lied to her.

She was still reeling from whatever had happened to her love affair, and she was making a quixotic quest to New Orleans for reasons Pearce still hadn't deduced. Perhaps she herself really didn't know why.

He had to admit she was putting up an excellent front. She was trying to be a real Girl Scout, brave, helpful, trustworthy, considerate and cheerful. But, he thought grimly, she was an unseasoned traveler. She'd been nervous on the plane, confused by the delays, and he could tell she was scared now. She should be scared. Her money was probably gone for good, a complication she certainly didn't need.

And she seemed to have nobody to turn to, nobody to depend on—except himself and one old retired guide dog, short of breath and becoming arthritic.

He glanced at her out of the corner of his eye. He had vowed not to open his eyes this trip, but as soon as he'd heard her voice, he'd had to see her. He kept closing his eyes, and the voice kept making them open again.

She had a cute face, freckled and pert of nose. Her eyes were beautiful and so was the red-gold hair, which, he had to admit, he found glorious.

But she'd made it clear she had no use for liars.

It was obviously not the best time, Pearce thought, to tell her that he had twenty-twenty vision; that he had, in fact, phenomenal vision. He could see better than most people, probably better than Mollie.

What he saw, when he glanced down at her, was a pale-faced and breathless bundle of trouble.

Pearce Goddard had always loved trouble with all his reckless heart; he loved it as much as he loved his freedom, which was a great deal.

Someone had once quoted a line from a book, saying it described Pearce to a T: "He was born with the gift of laughter and a sense that the world was mad."

It was true. And trouble was the one thing in the world he couldn't resist. He found, staring at that red-gold hair, that he couldn't resist it now.

CHAPTER THREE

PEARCE HAD BEEN RIGHT about Mollie's purse. Some-body found it tossed into a far corner of a women's rest room and turned it in at the ticket desk. Her credit card, checks and identification were still inside. The money, all three hundred dollars, was gone. The airline allowed her to cash a check for fifty dollars. It was the only money she had.

Mollie stood, still numb, in the waiting area with Pearce, clutching the purse as hard as she could. How foolish to hang onto it tightly now, she thought, but she couldn't stop herself. The act was pure reflex.

The crowd at the gate had grown, and she and Pearce were pushed closely together. They stood so near she wondered if he could feel the hammering of heart, feel how the blood pounded through her body.

She was glad that he couldn't see her face. She knew she was pale and that no matter how steady she kept her expression, she couldn't hide the panic in her eyes.

"You double-checked?" he asked. Fritz was pressed against his legs, panting. The crowd was beginning to buffet the dog, but it stood patiently, refusing to budge from its master. "They got all the money? But all your credit cards are there?"

"Yes," Mollie said. Her hair had started coming loose from its barrette and hung in red-gold tendrils around her face. "All the money. And I only have one credit card...my father never believed in them. He says you shouldn't spend what you haven't got.''

Pearce nodded, but the set of his mouth was sardonic, bitterly amused. "A wise man. Unless, of course, his wallet ever gets stolen. Well, the credit card should take care of you. You can charge your hotel bill, and most good restaurants take them.''

"But...'' she protested, shaking her head. She blinked hard, trying to control her tumbling emotions and think more clearly.

"I...'' She paused, then straightened her spine. "He's right. My father, I mean. I shouldn't be spending what I haven't got. Do you suppose they'd cash in my ticket? That they'd led me fly back to New York?''

"No,'' Pearce said flatly. "Don't even try. That's not how airlines work. Even if you tried to go back now, you could only get a seat on standby. Which means you could wait here for damned ever. You could spend Christmas *and* New Year's stranded in Dallas. And probably Groundhog Day and the Fourth of July, too. No. You're better off going to New Orleans.''

"But—'' Mollie objected, then couldn't finish the sentence. If the thief had struck her on the head as well as robbed her, she couldn't have been left more confused.

Pearce's expression grew more sardonic still. "I know. You don't want to go into debt.'' His smile went crooked. "What's your father do, anyway? Is he a preacher? A professor? Or just a homegrown philosopher?''

Mollie looked at him in surprise. He was excellent at guessing things, far too perceptive, and she hoped he didn't guess her mood. She managed to keep her voice controlled, confident. "He's a professor. How did you know?''

He shrugged, lifted one eyebrow. His mouth took on a slight smile and his drawl became slower and more mocking than usual. "You've also got that air about you. Independent. Forthright. An air of very definitely putting up with no nonsense. And—maybe—a little afraid of having fun."

She blinked again, this time in surprise. How could he have gotten such an idea? "Me? Afraid of having fun? Never."

She had always been the most playful, imaginative one in her family. She was far more full of jokes and teasing and mischief than Michael, who was almost always serious. She had never been afraid to kick up her heels, either at home or in college. Her heart gave a small, painful lurch. *But what about since college?* All she'd done was work, breaking her back to pursue a career and survive in New York.

Somebody jostled Mollie so she was pushed more closely toward Pearce, and he put his arm around her to keep her steady. His mouth turned down at one corner. "When's the last time you had a good time?"

She was pressed so near to him, nestled so securely in the crook of his arm, that it gave her an odd sensation, as if the strength were melting out of her thighs. She stared into his dark glasses without comprehension, her heart beating fast. She tried to concentrate on his question, not on the effect he was having on her body.

When had she last had a good time? She supposed it was last Christmas. She had gone home to Minnesota and spent the holidays with her family. Michael had his own family to visit and papers to write for his classes, but they had managed to go skiing once, to the movies once and the theater three times. Yet the hours they had stolen together had always been intense, hurried, with no time to relax. What had been the most fun?

Musingly she remembered decorating the family tree and getting into a tinsel fight with her brother, Hamilton. The fight went wild, moving outside and escalating until somehow her sister Ruth got into it, too. The three of them found themselves in the largest and most outrageous snowball fight in family history. She and Ruth had mercilessly pelted Hamilton into submission, finally throwing him into a snowbank and sitting on him. It had been glorious.

She smiled at the memory, a slow, half-sad smile. How odd, she mused; the last time she'd had fun was with her family, not with Michael. And just as oddly, Michael had never made her heart beat as erratically as did this man she was now pressed against, a man she hardly knew. She didn't know what to say.

"Well," Pearce said sarcastically. "Does it take you that long to remember having fun?" His lean fingers toyed with the collar of her trench coat and she could feel his breath stirring the loosened strands of her hair.

"No," she said softly. "I was thinking of last Christmas, that's all." She tried to step away from him, because his touch was doing things to her that she couldn't deal with now, not after all that had happened. She found she couldn't move far; the crowd was jammed too thickly.

He must have sensed her disturbance because he took his arm away, but the black glasses kept staring down at her, unreadable and impassive. The corner of his mouth twitched downward again. He gave a short, derisive nod. "A year. You remember having fun a year ago."

She opened her purse distractedly, trying to ignore his implication by making sure her billfold and credit card hadn't disappeared again. Pearce was only increasing her unease and she was still filled with a roiling, restless sickness from the theft.

Perhaps the worst thing about being robbed, she thought, nonplussed, was not the loss of money. The worst thing was loss of trust. Before she had looked on the crowd around her as fellow travelers, kindred souls. Now any one of them might be the thief. It was neither a cheering thought nor a charitable one to have at Christmas. Since Michael, she had little enough faith in humanity to spare.

"Mollie," Pearce demanded, twin frown lines appearing above the nosepiece of his glasses, "are you listening to me? Can you honestly say you really haven't had fun for a full year?"

She shut the purse again and clutched it to her. She shrugged. He was right. She hadn't really enjoyed herself for a year. But why? After all, she'd been in love, and what was a more enjoyable sensation than being in love? Perhaps she hadn't been as much in love with Michael as she'd thought.

Pearce bent his face nearer to hers. His mouth curved almost seductively. "You owe it to yourself to go to New Orleans. Because New Orleans is always a feast and always a carnival and always a party. Don't turn back now. Show some courage."

Affronted, she stood even straighter. "I've got plenty of courage. It's not a question of courage. It's one of economics. I've only got two part-time jobs lined up back in New York. I just can't afford to go to New Orleans. Not now."

"You can't afford not to go." His voice was soft, beguiling. "Before it was only a vacation. Now it's an adventure."

She looked at him in disbelief. "You can call this an adventure? It's a *disaster.*"

"Adventures always flirt with disaster," he said with the same wicked smile. "If they didn't, they wouldn't be adventures, would they? Money? You can always get more money. You've got the rest of your life to make money. But you'll never get this Christmas in New Orleans again. You've got only one chance at it. Take it. What fun would life be if we never took chances?"

She stared up at him, her heart beating harder than before. He was right. She had taken chances when she'd gone to New York, taken chances when she'd chosen acting for a career. Michael had been the one afraid of adventure, not she.

An unexpected thrill of excitement burned through her nerves. So what if she lived on credit for a few days? It was hardly a sin. She had already found someone back in New York who would sublease her apartment after the first of the year—Clytie, bless her, had known of someone searching for just such an apartment. Mollie's finances were tight, but they were not yet desperate.

"Well?" Pearce drawled, his eyebrows arching even higher.

She took a deep breath. "I'll go," she said.

THEIR PLANE WAS DELAYED twice more and they didn't arrive in New Orleans until after one o'clock. They had plenty of time for small talk, comfortable and without direction.

Mollie told Pearce about growing up in Minnesota and trying to break into acting in New York. He told her in turn that he'd grown up in a small town west of Austin, Texas, but now lived in California. For a living, he said rather vaguely, he did something in entertainment. He

mentioned just as vaguely that it had to do—sort of—
with children.

Children's entertainment? Stories? Mollie had thought
in surprise. He hardly seemed the type. There was something too unquestionably male about him to imagine him
writing stories about talking bunnies and choo-choo
trains, but when she tried to question him further, he
neatly dodged answering.

Neither of them talked about their relationships, past
or present, with anyone of the opposite sex. Pearce
seemed to avoid the topic as completely as she did. By the
time they landed in New Orleans, they knew dozens of
trivial facts about each other and few important ones.

Now, on the ground at last, Mollie held Pearce's arm
and told him how to get to the baggage claim area. Fritz
paced along swiftly, but his ears were drooping and he
was panting again.

"Is he all right?" Mollie asked with concern. "He
looks tired."

"All he needs is a good night's sleep," Pearce assured
her. "He's tough."

Mollie wasn't sure. She wondered just how strong the
old dog really was, but she didn't voice her doubts. She
looked about instead. "What a strange airport," she re-
marked. "The walls are covered with posters—I've never
seen so many. There's one everywhere you look—for the
Mardi Gras or some other kind of festival. I've never
heard of so many festivals."

"Louisiana's the festival capital of the continent," he
said. "There's always one someplace. Any reason's good
enough for a party. They even have a 'possum festival.
You know the state motto—the unofficial one?"

"No," Mollie said. "What?"

"Laissez les bons temps rouler," he answered. "It's French. Let the good times roll. And in New Orleans, they believe in doing just that."

Mollie's eyes searched the crowd. This airport wasn't nearly as busy as the one in Dallas, but most of the people looked just as tired and frustrated. She felt tired and frustrated herself, but she struggled to stay cheerful because somehow Pearce's spirits never flagged.

What a valiant man, she thought with a surge of admiration. What a brave, high-spirited and unique man he was, moving undaunted through his world of darkness. He met every trouble as a challenge. She would try to do the same. He had helped her every step along the way. She only wished she would have a chance to help him half as much in return.

PEARCE GODDARD ALMOST always found trouble interesting, but this trip, he thought grimly, was beginning to turn into too much of a good thing.

It was two o'clock in the morning and their luggage was lost.

No, it wasn't exactly lost, the bleary-eyed baggage clerk told the crowd of passengers who had stood for over an hour waiting for their bags.

What their luggage actually was was *frozen.* The temperature had fallen to two above zero in semitropical New Orleans, thirty degrees below freezing. The luggage hold of the plane, aided by some mechanical failures, had frozen shut with such iron tightness that nobody could pry it open without damaging the plane.

The crowd around the luggage carousel stirred angrily at the announcement, the faces dangerously surly. The clerk looked nervous. "If you can just be patient," he began, "we'll give you a toll-free number to call."

"This is ridiculous," Pearce hissed. Things were so quirky and unpredictable tonight he suspected that the fates were celebrating the holidays early, had overdone it and were drunk and irresponsible as skunks.

Opening his eyes, he stole a glance at Mollie. Her face had gone blank at the announcement, but she kept her shoulders squared and her chin up. Now she was in New Orleans without money and without luggage. And he had an ominous feeling that it might be a long time before either of them saw their suitcases again.

"I don't understand," she said, shaking her head so that the light glinted in her fiery hair. "Our luggage is here, but they can't get to it? What's going to happen?"

"I don't like the sound of this," he said, his teeth clenched. "Not at all."

Mollie's eyes widened in alarm. "What's wrong?"

He cast her another furtive look from behind his dark glasses. Hell, he thought, she was a trooper. He'd give her the straight truth.

"They're giving us a toll-free number. That means it's long distance. And that means trouble. It's not the usual procedure. They should be taking down our addresses. If your luggage is delayed, it's the airline's responsibility to deliver it to you. But they're not worried about that at this point. No. Those bags are going to be gone a while. We may not see them for days."

He watched her blue eyes haze over in shock. He allowed himself to touch her arm in encouragement. She was an eminently touchable woman, warm and filled with quick emotions. She could be dangerous if he allowed it.

She gave him a slightly sick smile that she thought he couldn't see. "Then what's happening?"

He resisted the sudden desire to put his finger under her chin, lift her face, kiss her and say, "Life's happening. Let's make the most of it." He didn't know where the impulse came from. It was probably a good thing they were parting soon.

"What's happening," he said with mock carelessness, "is that our luggage is stuck inside that plane—and the plane has to take off for somewhere else. Did you ever ask what its final destination was?"

"No," she said warily. "Where is it?"

He set his mouth at a wry angle. "Yucatán. Our luggage is going to Yucatán. Let's hope it has a pleasant trip."

"Yucatán?" she cried in horror. "That's in Central America!"

"*Si, señorita,*" he said sarcastically. "Indeed it is." He put his hand on her arm again. "Look. Let's skip standing in line to get a phone number that can't help us tonight anyway. It's late. You're tired, I'm tired, the dog's tired. We can call tomorrow and check this out. Let's get out of here. Is your hotel in the French Quarter? We can share a cab."

Mollie's face went so pale that her freckles stood out on her cheekbones like faint brown spangles. She said nothing. Her expression was stricken.

Lady, Pearce thought darkly, *please don't have any more bad luck.*

He gripped her arm more tightly. She opened her mouth several times before she could speak. "I can't...exactly remember the address of my hotel. I—I'm not too sure about the name, even. It's Jefferson or Jackson or Johnson or something like that. Oh, good heavens. How stupid."

Pearce's brows drew together. She was right; it was stupid, even though she wasn't a stupid girl. How could she do such a thing?

"Didn't you write it down?" he asked in disbelief.

She nodded. Her hair had come completely undone now, and it bobbed in red-gold confusion around her face. "Of course, I wrote it down. I was very careful to write it down. I put it in the notebook where I keep all my important information."

He made an impatient gesture with his wide shoulders. "Good Lord, did you forget to bring the book?"

"Of course, I brought it," she almost wailed. "It's in my suitcase." She slapped her forehead in dismay. "I wasn't thinking clearly. Oh, I wasn't thinking at all—everything's been so... awful lately. What was wrong with me? *What?*"

She groaned, inwardly damning herself for such a mindless act. She damned Michael, too, for reducing her to such a state that she blundered about doing such asinine things. Why had she packed the notebook? Why had it never occurred to her her luggage might be lost?

Pearce must think she was an idiot. He'd be right, she told herself, she *was* an idiot. How could she have lost the name and address of her hotel? A moment's thoughtlessness, and now she was marooned.

She looked so upset, so angry and unhappy with herself that Pearce felt a surge of concern. A plan formed in his fertile brain, a plan that was slightly wicked, but amusing.

"I'll go through a phone book," she said with desperate determination. "I'll figure out which hotel it was. I'm sure it's Jackson or Jefferson or something like that."

He took a deep breath. "Mollie," he said with elaborate casualness, "half of New Orleans is named 'Jackson.' Did you send any money for a deposit on that room?"

"No." She looked at him questioningly. "They didn't ask me to. Why?"

A muscle danced in his tanned cheek. "Because they're probably not even saving your room for you. It's two in the morning. When you didn't show up, they probably rented it to somebody else—it's normal procedure. Every travel arrangement in this town is turned upside down. It's going to be a madhouse."

"Oh, *great,*" she said bitterly. "Well, so be it. I'll help you get a cab, and I'll sleep in the airport. I deserve it. I think I just won the gold medal for brainless traveling. In fact, I probably qualified for the Hall of Fame. I'll find a place tomorrow. It's not that long until morning."

He stood a moment, his dark glasses staring off pensively into space, as if some inner combat were taking place within him. At last he spoke.

"Mollie," he said solemnly, "I know it seems as if everything's gone wrong for you. But maybe somebody's watching out for me. I'll admit something to you."

He paused, and the pause was full of reluctant emotion. "I hate to admit this. I—I'm nervous about being on my own. My friend isn't here. I'm in a strange city. Why don't we stay together? You can share my room. Stay with me." He swallowed, hard. "Help me," he said gently.

He couldn't describe the look that crossed her face. "Stay with you?" she repeated, her voice slightly strangled.

He spoke as fast and convincingly as he could, his face earnest. He held his head high, as if he were a proud man unused to asking for favors. Pearce Goddard was an excellent actor; it was one small part of his job.

"We've helped each other this far, haven't we?" he asked, his voice earnest. "You haven't got a room. I haven't got anybody to guide me. I swear to you I'm not proposing anything...wrong, improper. Stay with me. Just for the night and maybe a while tomorrow. Help me get my bearings. Otherwise—it's like that line from that play—I can only depend on the kindness of strangers. Please."

Mollie hesitated. She looked up at him, then down at the dog. Fritz sat, ears drooping and tongue out, looking old, overweight and tired.

"I know I've got the dog," Pearce said, his drawl sounding suddenly tense. "But he's old. To tell the truth, he's too old. I know I have to replace him. I should have done it already. But I wanted to make one last trip with him, spend one last Christmas. Now I'm worried. Maybe I'm asking too much of the old guy. I've felt it tonight; he's tired. He's very tired. Mollie—won't you help us? Both of us?" He swallowed with suppressed emotion.

She kept staring down at Fritz. At last she lifted her face to Pearce's. She seemed lost in a complicated series of thoughts, and she studied his face so thoroughly that he took extra effort to look sincere, noble and entreating. She looked so deliciously thoughtful and concerned that he swallowed again.

Slowly she nodded. "All right," she said in her husky voice. "To help each other. There's nothing...romantic about it."

He shook his head. "Nothing at all," he agreed. He had no intention of becoming emotionally involved with her. He was in a position to help her, and he found it amusing to do so. If, however, she proved agreeable to a sexual liaison, who was he to deny her a desired pleasure?

"Thank you, Mollie," he said, his voice tight. "You're very kind."

"You're the one who's kind," she said, her face full of emotion. She took his arm. "Come on. Let's get a cab. You must be tired. The doors are to your left."

Pearce's conscience tweaked him when she took his arm with such kindly warmth. He told his conscience to take a hike. *Leave,* he said to the atypical twinge of guilt. "Left," he said to the dog.

Well, Pearce thought with a mental shrug, he could almost hear his uncle laughing now. Pearce had promised the old man, hadn't he? Faron had been blind, but he'd never lost his taste for devilment. He'd said, "When I die, I want you to do three things. First, use the money I leave you to make that fool movie. Second, on your way home from my funeral, flirt with the prettiest girl you can find. Third, take care of Fritz. That's all the memorial I want."

Pearce was going to New Orleans before he went home, and the decision to pretend to be blind was half playful, half practical. Although he was saddened by Faron's death, Faron had forbidden mourning, and recent events had put Pearce in a rash and heady mood. He was burning his bridges behind him, getting ready to take a hell of a chance.

Besides, he had told himself, there'd been the very real problem of transporting the dog. The airline would let Fritz ride in the passenger section only if he was working as a guide dog. Otherwise he would be caged and put in the hold with the luggage. Which would mean, the way this trip was going, that the old dog would now have been trapped, cold, hungry, and on his unhappy way to Yucatán.

No, Pearce thought, glancing down at the red-gold tumble of Mollie's hair, he meant no harm pretending to be blind, and he could do the woman some good. She wouldn't come with him if she knew he could see. Continuing his mild deception, he convinced himself, was almost courtly. She was a damsel in distress. He had no choice but to continue the lie and play knight.

He closed his eyes again, cloaking himself in artificial blindness. It was his research. It was one of the things he had come to do and that he must do. Finding out how it felt to be blind was the one thing, without fail, that he had to do on this trip. *Stop looking at the girl,* he told himself, *and get on with the work.*

AT TWO O'CLOCK IN THE morning, when streets were slicked with ice, catching a cab in New Orleans was only slightly less difficult than capturing a unicorn.

Although Mollie had grown up with the deep snows of Minnesota and lived through the brutality of New York's long winter, she thought she had never been as cold as she was that night in New Orleans.

She was wearing a blue plaid wool skirt, a long-sleeved pink blouse over a dark blue turtleneck, knee-high boots and her trench coat, which, fortunately, had a zip-in lining she had worn to ward off the cold on the way to the New York airport. But her gloves were thin, her knit cap didn't cover her ears, and she couldn't stop shivering even after she and Pearce got into the warm interior of the cab.

Pearce, who wore only a medium weight jacket and had no hat or gloves, must be even colder than she, she thought, although he seemed far less sensitive to the cold. Fritz sat on the cab's floor, which was damp with melted ice and slush. He closed his eyes miserably and shuddered from time to time.

The cab driver, a hyperactive man who told them he had migrated to New Orleans from New Jersey, said that most of the native Southern cab drivers had given up trying to drive on the unfamiliar ice. Too many accidents, he said, and so many skids and collisions on one icy bridge that the bridge had been closed for public safety.

"Nope," the driver said genially, "nobody out tonight but Yankees and crazy people. Which one are you people?"

Mollie gave another involuntary shiver. Pearce put a comforting arm around her, and she was too cold and tired to protest.

"She's a Yankee," Pearce said amiably. "I'm crazy."

"Ha!" chortled the driver. "I'm both." And he took a corner at such speed that the cab slid and veered from one curb to the other. "I love havin' the streets to myself. Watch—if you hit the brakes fast, it's like skatin'."

Mollie shuddered harder than before and closed her eyes.

"Don't be afraid," Pearce whispered comfortingly, making her ear tingle. "If he kills us instantly, at least we'll die warm."

The driver laughed again and skidded around another corner. "Mush!" he cried happily. "Mush, you huskies, mush!"

What if he doesn't kill us instantly? Mollie wanted to ask. *What if he crashes and we freeze to death lying in the streets?* She squeezed her eyes tightly shut as the driver skated, skidded, and very nearly tobogganed them to their destination.

When the cab drew up before the hotel, her knees were shaking slightly as she got out. The night air bit into her, chilling her to the marrow once more. She felt numb and slightly unreal as Pearce checked them in at the night clerk's desk. Things seemed to be happening to her as in a dream.

The hotel looked both expensive and venerable to her dazed eyes, its lobby posh. Elaborate chandeliers hung from the ceiling, the most ornate Mollie had ever seen. The polished wood of antique furniture gleamed in the golden light of the chandeliers, and the velvet upholstery in deep blue and crimson was so rich it almost shimmered.

Several huge Christmas trees had been erected about the room. The trees, flocked with white, stood almost ceiling tall, festooned with red velvet bows, artificial birds with scarlet feathers, and fragile heart-shaped baubles of red and white china. Mollie had never seen trees more beautiful except in the Christmas windows of the stores on Fifth Avenue.

She sucked in her breath in wonder. This was a fine hotel, probably one of the finest and most expensive in New Orleans. The one she would have stayed in was the opposite, one of the least expensive. It would have been nothing like this, nothing.

She suddenly felt guilty for accepting such lodgings from Pearce. He had promised that he expected nothing in return except her help, but what if he reneged on his promise?

She trembled with cold again. No, she had to trust him. Somehow she would have to reimburse him for sharing this luxury. But how? Who knew how long she'd have to work to pay for this vacation as it was?

The night clerk dropped the keys into Pearce's hand. Pearce turned to her. "Ready?" he asked and offered her his arm. She stared about the lobby, with its Victorian nooks and crannies, its randomly arranged furniture, its two large curving staircases.

It would be nearly impossible for a blind man, even with a dog, to make his way safely to the staircase and find his destination without human help. She could understand Pearce's reluctance to depend on desk clerks or bellboys to lead him about. He was a proud man. It was natural he found it more tolerable to ask one person for help than depend on whatever stranger was at hand.

She lifted her chin in determination and took his arm.

"Room 242," he said with a slanted smile, holding the key out to her. "And at least we don't have to bother with the luggage. It's probably halfway to Yucatán by now."

Room 242 seemed almost as luxurious as the lobby to Mollie. Silvery blue silk wallpaper was striped with a darker blue that matched the thick carpet and the heavy velvet drapes. Oil paintings in gilded frames hung on the walls above Queen Anne furniture, and fresh white roses were arranged in crystal vases on the end tables beside the velvet-covered settee.

"It's beautiful," Mollie breathed as she pulled the door shut behind them.

"Is it?" Pearce said cryptically. "Show me how to get around in it, will you?"

She winced, wondering if he found her insensitive for marveling at beauty that he couldn't see. She walked him around the room and the adjoining bathroom, telling him where everything was located.

The last thing she showed him was the bed. It was a king-size bed with four ornately carved posts and a silvery blue satin spread.

"Here," she said. "Sit down. It's your bed. It looks wonderful." She tried to release him, but he kept her arm clamped firmly beneath his own and laced his fingers through hers.

"Does it?" he asked with a quirk of his brow. "You take it. I'll sleep on the settee."

Her fingers tingled at his touch, and strange frissons raced through her arm and up and down her spine. She couldn't let him give up his bed. And she couldn't let him touch her so, but for some reason she did not resist. "No," she objected. "I will. You couldn't. It's too short."

"Only a cad would let a woman sleep on the settee. You take the bed. I insist. Here. Sit."

He drew her down to the bed until the two of them were sitting together on its satin edge, her arm still linked through his. She tried to rise. "I really wouldn't feel right—"

Gently but firmly, he held her beside him, not letting her move away. "I'll let you sleep where you want if you'll do one thing for me." His drawl was low and husky.

"What?" Mollie asked with trepidation. She remembered how flirtatious Pearce could be when he chose, and she wasn't sure she could deal with it. She was already shaken by the stolen money, the lost luggage and the wild cab ride.

"I want to touch your face," he said, bringing one hand first to her shoulder, then to graze her cheek. His fingers hovered against her face, barely touching it. Their closeness, their warmth, was maddening. "May I?"

She licked her lips nervously. Wasn't that how blind people learned how another person looked? By touching the person's face? In one sense it seemed a friendly, reasonable request. In another, it sent apprehensions of danger dancing through her. Michael, she suddenly realized, had been a boy. Pearce Goddard was a man, one who made her senses flutter drunkenly.

"Please," he said, bending so near that she felt his breath tickle and softly burn her lips.

"I...don't think I should," she said and tried to rise again, but his other hand tightened on her arm, holding her fast beside him.

She didn't struggle to escape. She seemed held in place by some magic spell, helpless to resist. She drew in her breath as his fingertips touched her jawline, rose slowly and traced first the line of her eyebrow, then the silky line of her cheekbone.

"Long eyelashes," he said softly, his fingertip grazing them. She shut her eyes and let his fingers explore her lids with butterfly softness. His touch radiated power, yet it was gentle, too, the deftest touch she had ever felt.

"A smooth brow," he said, stroking it beneath the tendrils of loose hair. "And a pert little nose. It must one of those cute Scandinavian Minnesotan noses. And a firm little chin. Stubborn, but not unreasonably so."

The emotions that Mollie had been trying to freeze for the last two weeks suddenly thawed and swarmed through her tired body. The feelings she had tried to stifle since she had first stepped on the plane broke free and stormed her tired mind.

It feels good for him to touch me, she thought with tremulous dreaminess. *It feels so right. Nobody ever touched me this way before.*

"And your mouth," he breathed, drawing his thumb across it with lingering tenderness. "Your mouth is full. And soft. And ripe."

His hand moved to frame her jaw, and he tilted her face up toward his. "Your mouth," he said, bending nearer, "is like your voice—mysterious. It takes special investigating. May I?"

Then he did what Mollie had secretly wanted him to do from the moment she first saw him, with his dark glasses and his fascinating, unreadable mouth.

He pressed his lips to hers and kissed her as she'd never been kissed in her life.

CHAPTER FOUR

HIS MOUTH ON HERS WAS warm, mobile and sensuous. The hands that gripped her arms were compelling in their strength and sureness. For the first time in weeks, Mollie's body pulsed with the excitement of being alive, and her blood quickened almost joyously at his touch.

The high, thick wall she had built around her emotions vanished as if it had been nothing more substantial than a wisp of smoke. She had been as one half-dead, floating in some dim limbo, but as he wrapped his arms around her waist, kissing her more deeply still, the vital spirit sparked brightly within her once again. She had been cold, but his questing mouth warmed her like a life-giving fire.

His lips had always looked intriguing to her, promising all sorts of contradictions. Now their touch tantalized her, hinting at those same contradictions. There was hunger in his caress, but an unexpected gentleness, too, that filled her with a deep, aching longing. Something of both the pirate and the poet stirred in his kiss, something of both the rogue and the rhapsodist.

She sighed softly against his mouth, gladly sharing the life he seemed to be pouring into her. She had an odd, sweet sense of having come home and wanted to put her arms around his neck. How lovely it would be to lose herself in his strange mixture of coolness and fire. To truly come home at last.

But you're not home, she thought, the words cutting like ice through the warmth that suffused her. She was a long way from home, in a strange city, a strange room and in a stranger's arms. Suddenly she felt cold again, cold to the bone with shock at what she was doing.

She would have sprung away from him had he not held her so tightly. She pulled back as abruptly as she could. "Stop that," she hissed, pushing against his chest. In the lenses of his dark glasses she saw twin images of herself, pale and with her hair in a red-gold tumble.

His upper lip curled at one corner. "But we were being such a comfort to each other."

She clamped her mouth shut in disgust and pushed at his chest again, her heart stormy. What was wrong with her? Why had she felt attracted to him? It was insane. She knew nothing about him.

Unsettled, she wondered if she had kissed him merely because of Michael. This night was to have been her wedding night. Was some dark impulse driving her to have a honeymoon with a handsome stranger, since she no longer had a groom? Had she kissed Pearce only because she wanted to forget Michael—or to spite him?

"Steady," Pearce said between his teeth. "And don't sound so furious. You enjoyed it. Or is that what makes you furious?"

"Let go of me," she ordered.

"Only if you promise not to run. First, you don't have anyplace to run to. Second, when I started to kiss you, all you had to do was say no."

"I'm saying no now," Mollie said through gritted teeth. She struggled to get away from him, but she realized she was not struggling hard or even with much conviction. There was something she liked about being in his arms, although she knew feeling so was wrong. It was all the more reason to escape.

He smiled tautly, raising his eyebrows in resignation. "All right," he said. "First you were willing, but now you're not. A man never knows."

With a fatalistic sigh, he released her. "I'll sleep on the settee." He bent, groping for the handle of Fritz's harness. Fritz was staring up at the two of them with something eerily akin to disapproval in his eyes.

Mollie stood, stepping back from the bed. "*I'll* sleep on the settee," she said, jabbing a thumb at her own chest. "You said I could choose where I sleep, and that's where I choose."

Pearce, too, had stood, his face as unconcerned as if they were discussing the weather. Mollie took another step away from him, just to be on the safe side.

"If you make another pass at me," she warned, her voice shaking with emotion, "you'll be sorry. I'll yell and scream and break things. And when the police come, I'll tell them you lured me up here under false pretenses. You promised you wouldn't try anything. You said you needed my help. Behave yourself or I'll walk right out on you—after I make a fuss they'll hear clear to Mississippi."

An expression of disgust mingled with amusement crossed his features. "You'd abandon me?"

"In a minute," Mollie said with a snap of her fingers to emphasize how fast. "So keep your promise. Or else."

He sighed again, dropping the dog's harness, and threw himself back down on the bed. He put his hands behind his head and kept his face turned toward the ceiling. "Sleep in the bathtub if you like. As for breaking a promise, *please* forgive me."

He said "Please forgive me" with such sarcasm that it rankled Mollie, making her put her hands on her hips.

"You weren't exactly running away screaming," he said, his voice ironic. "You sat on the bed with me, not really protesting—"

"I did so pro—" Mollie began, but he cut her off impatiently.

"Without *really* protesting. When I kissed you, you kissed me back. With enthusiasm, I might add. Then you changed your mind. That's the problem with women. They tell you one thing, but they want another. They say no when they mean yes. They say yes when they mean no. How's a man supposed to know unless he tries?"

"Don't try to blame this on me," Mollie warned, but in truth she felt guilty. Had she invited his advances, unconsciously or perhaps even consciously? She could have stepped firmly away from the bed instead of consenting to sit beside him. She could have refused to let him touch her face. When he bent to kiss her, she could have turned away. But she had not. Had she perhaps even lifted her face to him so his lips would find hers more easily?

"I'm not blaming anybody." His tone was mocking. "And you've made yourself clear. I won't steal up on you in the night, trying to force my evil intentions on you. I've got no taste for that kind of thing. There are plenty of women in the world that don't have to be begged or be forced. Believe me."

He yawned lavishly, covering his mouth in a parody of politeness. Mollie stared at him, conflicting emotions crowding her chest, making her breathe hard. He was stretched out long and lean on the silver-blue coverlet, and he gave a voluptuous sigh of comfort. Surrounded by that sea of pale blue, he looked more tanned and fit than ever, his brown hair almost dark.

He seemed to have forgotten any thought he might have given Mollie, and she wondered if what he'd said was true: he'd tried to make love to her out of mere curiosity. She hadn't been willing, so he was no longer interested. She had a strong instinct that this time he would be true to his word. He would approach her no more.

She moved to the settee and sat down, still staring at him. She felt a vague, inexplicable disappointment, as if some sort of vivifying excitement had left her life.

Heavens, she thought reluctantly, maybe it was simply because he was such a good-looking man. His handsomeness was far different from Michael's. Michael's was more refined, almost pretty. Pearce Goddard had no trace of prettiness about him. His face was all hard planes and masculine curves, just like his tall body, but what was most fascinating about him was the mercurial swiftness with which he could change from one mood to another.

He yawned again. He rose to a sitting position, groped for Fritz, unharnessed him and hung the harness over the bedpost. Then he lay down again, once more stretching out his hands behind his head. "Good night, sweet lady. That's a line from a play, isn't it? 'Good night, good night, good night.' Make yourself comfy."

His expression was slightly smug and extremely bored. Mollie looked away from him in frustration. He might be blind, but he had the audacity and confidence of five men.

She sighed, rose and began searching for an extra pillow and blankets. She found them in one of the room's two closets and made herself a sort of nest on the settee.

Glancing again at Pearce she saw he was breathing deeply and regularly, as if sleep had already claimed him. The dog lay curled beside the bed, its graying muzzle tucked against its tail. Once again it snored. Once again she heard the turgid gurgling of its digestion.

Mollie crossed the room to turn off the lights. Just as her hand touched the lamp switch, Pearce spoke again.

"He probably isn't worth it, you know." His words startled her. She had been certain he was asleep. She stood as if paralyzed, her hand still touching the switch.

"Who isn't worth it?" Reluctantly she allowed herself to gaze at him again, but his expressive face was blank, his dark glasses still in place, masking his eyes.

"Whoever he is," Pearce said lazily. "The guy you're grieving for. He isn't worth it. You'll forget him—the sooner the better."

Mollie drew in her breath and held it. How had he known? Was her predicament that obvious, even to a blind man? She swallowed and decided to ignore his statement. "Shouldn't you take your glasses off?" she asked.

"I will," he said, but made no move to do so. "Later."

She watched him a moment longer. Perhaps with the glasses off, she thought, he wasn't so handsome. Perhaps he had been disfigured somehow and didn't want her to see his scars. She felt a sudden flood of sympathy for him, in spite of everything.

She switched off the lamp and made her way across the thick carpet to the bathroom. Closing the door behind her, she turned on the light and tried to take stock of her situation.

She had no nightgown, no extra clothes at all, nothing. She took off her boots, paused a moment, then shed her pleated skirt, her blouse, her turtleneck and her panty hose. She would sleep in her bra and half-slip. What did it matter? Pearce couldn't see her.

She drew off her panties, too, and washed them, along with her hose, in the shell-shaped sink of veined blue marble. She hung them near the radiator to dry, glad that at least she would have a few clean clothes for tomorrow. She hung her other clothes on a hook on the back of the door, and set her boots neatly in the corner.

She washed her face and hands, then opened the door again, switching off the bathroom light. Fritz snored stentoriously in the dark. Silently she crossed the room, lowered herself to the settee and snuggled into the cramped little bed she'd made, pulling the blankets up around her chin.

What had Pearce meant? she wondered. How could he say that she'd forget Michael? How could she? She would remember Michael forever, she would miss him forever, he would haunt her forever.

When, however, she fell into exhausted sleep, it was not Michael who awaited her in her dreams. Instead she had a long, complicated, difficult dream about the Dallas airport. She was trying to make her way through its corridors, hanging onto the arm of a tall man with dark glasses and an intriguing mouth. Somehow she felt she could depend on this man, trust him as she had never trusted anyone.

YOU'RE NOT DEPENDABLE and nobody should ever trust you, Irina had angrily told Pearce. Then she'd called him several names that ladies weren't even supposed to know, let alone utter, and had hung up on him.

He supposed the girl curled on the settee would agree with Irina if she knew the truth about him. But Mollie Randall needed help, he told himself, and he'd been the only person around to offer it. That was that. Pragmatism, pure and simple.

He lay in the darkness, his eyes closed. He was tempted to raise up on his elbow and steal a glance at her in the moonlight that fell through the sheer curtains of the room's big window. But he did not. He was supposed to be blind this trip, a fact the girl kept making him forget.

He shouldn't have kissed her, that he knew. He shouldn't have looked at her, not even once. But as soon as she'd sat down beside him in the plane, her arm lightly brushing his, and spoken in that husky, velvet voice, he'd had to see her.

So, although he'd vowed not to open his eyes this trip, he had opened them. And there she'd sat. She had the most glorious mane of red-gold hair he'd ever seen, a face that was pretty in a wholesome, freckled sort of way, and although the way she held herself was proud and confident, there was sadness in her expressive blue eyes.

She made him want to write a poem:

Oh, why are you sad,
Beautiful, freckled girl with sunset hair?
Let me make you smile again.

He'd finally managed to close his eyes again, but he found he kept opening them to catch another glimpse of her. He'd been doing it all night long. Fascinating. Well, Faron had told him to flirt with the prettiest girl he could find on the way back from the funeral, and how was a man to know if a girl was pretty if he couldn't open his eyes?

He'd managed to keep his eyes shut while they were on the flight from Texas to New Orleans, but when they'd lost their luggage and she couldn't remember her hotel, he'd heard that lovely voice of hers—always so controlled—almost begin to shake with emotion. He couldn't help himself; he'd yielded to temptation again.

She'd looked so troubled, so full of anguish and remorse at her mistake, he'd had that familiar old what-the-hell feeling and had talked her into staying with him. Anything for a laugh; that had always been his motto before the disaster with Irina. It might as well be again.

He'd gone back to being blind in the cab and in the hotel lobby, but when she'd led him around the room and to the bed, he'd found himself opening his eyes again, hungry for another glimpse of her.

Now if a man was standing by a bed, arm in arm with a girl with fire both in her spirit and in her marvelous hair, what would a normal, red-blooded male do? Especially when he saw, hiding deep in her eyes, loneliness and want?

It had struck him, most forcibly, that she was in serious need of kissing. It struck him with equal force that he desired to touch that charmingly freckled face, to kiss those full lips, to run his hands through that rumpled red-gold hair. So he did. He kissed her.

He was not inexperienced. He knew when a woman liked being kissed, and this one did; she liked it a great deal. Her problem was that she didn't *want* to like it. And when she'd drawn away so abruptly, he'd found himself looking at her again.

Her chin had assumed a stubborn angle and anger flashed in her eyes, anger at both herself and him. She knew what they were doing was foolhardy.

Suddenly so did he. After all, he had the woman in his room under a false premise. If she had been willing to find warmth and consolation in his bed, no questions asked, no promises made, that was one thing. But if she protested, that was another thing completely. He needed to keep his hands off her, unless she signaled otherwise.

He sensed that her response to him had been as much a startling surprise to her as it was to him. Her lips had greeted his with a sweet hunger that had inflamed him. Her body had leaned against his as if it had been created for him to touch.

But they were strangers, he told himself sternly as he lay locked in his voluntary darkness. She was vulnerable, and he, for all his good intentions, was lying. She wasn't the sort of woman one lied to. And she wasn't the sort of woman one used casually and discarded. No, she was made for serious relationships, she was the kind a man got *involved* with, and the last thing on earth Pearce needed or wanted at this point in his life was to be involved.

He had nearly lost his freedom to Irina, and it had been a close escape. He was on the brink of taking the biggest gamble of his life, and his blood was running high. He was ready to embark on an adventure in which he could lose everything he had—or win everything he'd ever dreamed of. It was, in short, a time of extreme risk and no time to become *involved*.

Still, he wouldn't mind keeping the woman around. Her voice, for one thing. Her voice inspired him. His plan was to make a feature-length animated film, something as elaborate and ambitious as the early Disney features, the great ones, the kind nobody made anymore. He knew most of his characters, but he didn't yet know all of their voices.

When he'd heard hers, he knew he'd found one of the right ones. His hero was a rather pompous mole named Moncrief who was a detective, but, of course, being a mole, Moncrief was blind. Moncrief Mole, dark glasses, seeing-eye caterpillar and all, would come to New Orleans to solve the mysterious abduction of a beautiful young mink.

Pearce could see and hear most of the film in his head, but it was the mink, a central character, who had always been elusive, whose voice he could never hear. Until tonight.

Lulu the Mink needed to sound sexy but vulnerable, world-weary but innocent, sure of herself yet somehow just a hint uncertain. She should sound, in short, very much like Mollie Randall. The longer Mollie Randall was around, the more clearly Pearce could imagine Lulu.

Besides, he thought, shifting restlessly on the big bed, he could use help. Pretending to be blind in a strange town was no easy task, even with the dog. He'd thought he'd have Melissa with him, and Melissa, always game for anything, wouldn't have minded playing along with him while he was paying the bills.

He hungered to understand what it was like to be blind so he could get inside the mole's character, the mole's body, the mole's every movement and reaction. Pearce was an animator, one of California's best. All good animators were artists, but, like the great Disney himself, they were natural actors as well, becoming one with their characters.

All right, he told himself grimly. He'd indulged himself enough. It was time to get to work. From now on he had to live the part far better than he'd been doing so far. He couldn't allow the girl to keep tempting him to open his eyes. Nor could he let her get away. She was too important to his work.

But from here on out, he had to force himself to stay in darkness. He would not again allow himself to stare at that mass of red-gold hair, that spirited but lonely face.

He would not.

MOLLIE AWOKE BEFORE Pearce because the settee was too short and narrow to be a comfortable sleeping place. Groggily she raised herself on her elbow and looked across the room.

Cold light fell through the sheer curtains covering the window and the room was chilly. Fritz the dog still lay curled up faithfully by Pearce's bedside. His yellowish brown eyes were open, regarding Mollie with unwavering scrutiny, as if she might try something suspect.

Stretched out, half-wrapped in the silvery blue coverlet, Pearce lay on his side, one bare arm thrown out. She found once more that she could not keep from staring at him.

He had taken off his sweater and shirt sometime during the night; they hung from one of the bedposts. She could see one of his knees thrusting from beneath the bedclothes and knew that he still wore his slacks. But his upper body was naked, bronzed and gleaming against the coverlet.

She nibbled her lip in unconscious nervousness as she studied him. He had what she thought of as a swimmer's body, all sculpted muscle and with a stomach as flat and hard as a washboard. His chest was shadowy with curly brown hair tapering to a dark line that ran down his stomach and disappeared somewhere beneath the cover of quilted satin.

His eyes were closed. The skin around them was slightly less tan than the rest of his face, from always wearing the dark glasses, she supposed. Now the glasses lay folded on the night table.

At last she could clearly see his brows, which were arched in a way that looked devilish even as he slept. Although laugh lines were deeply etched around his eyes, she saw no scars. His lashes were long for a man's, dark and curving.

He sighed, stirred and rolled over to his other side. The motion caused all of his bared muscles to ripple in a most thought-provoking way. Mollie turned her head away in embarrassment. She didn't need to have such thoughts at all, let alone have them provoked.

She got up quietly and slipped into the bathroom, hoping the water pipes were quiet so she could take a shower without waking Pearce. The warm water on her naked body felt delicious and invigorating in the morning's chilliness. She dried herself with one of the hotel's sinfully luxurious towels and resolutely dressed in the same clothes she'd worn yesterday.

She brushed her hair until it crackled, then realized with dismay that she had lost her barrette somewhere during the course of events. She would have to let her hair hang free, although there was so much of it that it was always a nuisance.

Michael had always nagged her to cut it, although her drama teacher had told her she would be a fool to do so. And at least the hair had served some purpose, because it was the reason she'd got the part of the unconscious Clarice in the soap opera. Her hair, the director had decided, looked extremely dramatic spread across the pillow.

Michael, she thought with a start as she blotted her lipstick. For once she had thought of Michael almost without a pang. What she had felt most intensely was a surge of resentment that he had always criticized her hair, when everyone else said it was her best feature.

She started to powder her nose, then stopped, staring into the mirror. *Today I might have been Mrs. Michael Inglestadt,* she thought, the idea hardly seeming real. But she wasn't Mrs. Anybody. She was still plain Mollie Jo Randall and she had spent the night with a stranger. The stranger was lying half-naked in the next room at this moment.

What would Michael think of her if he knew? she wondered in horror. What would her friends and teachers back in Minnesota think? *Remember Mollie Randall, who was supposed to get married at Christmas? Instead she picked up a stranger on a plane and spent the night in his hotel room.*

Mollie paled, but she looked her mirrored image resolutely in the eye. She had done nothing wrong. Her father always told her not to worry about what people thought as long as she believed she was doing the right thing.

She swallowed hard. Her father's advice was more easily given than practiced. She should have been a respectable married woman today, ready to work with her life partner to carve out their careers in acting.

Instead she was a single woman sheltered by the charity of a man she didn't know, a man who could be boldly seductive. It was like being *kept,* she thought, flinching with a severe twinge of midwestern conscience.

The confusion and irony of her situation hit her hard and painfully. Once more she cursed Michael for what he had done. What a way to spend Christmas, she thought. Jilted, lonely, and in a situation that looked as compromising as possible. Suddenly she wished she was home in Minnesota with her family. But this year there was no home and family. And Michael didn't love her anymore. He loved somebody else.

For the first time in weeks her formidable self-control cracked and she wept. She wept helplessly into the big, plush hotel towel.

Although she cried hard, the spell passed quickly. Then she felt clean and somehow relieved. It would be the last time she would ever cry for Michael. Somehow she knew that.

She washed her face, reapplied her makeup and squared her jaw. She had to get on with her life. On her way to New Orleans, she had lost her fiancé, her money and her luggage. In their place, she had acquired an amorous blind man and an arthritic German shepherd. So be it. She could handle it. She would make the most of it.

She straightened her clothes and put her hand on the knob to open the door. She paused, remembering how she had spent the night running in her dreams, reliving the crowded, frustrating obstacle course of the Dallas airport.

In those dreams she'd had a sense of perfect trust in Pearce Goddard. She shook her head at the oddness. Awake she didn't trust him at all. Why, in dreams, should she find him so strong, so totally dependable? It mystified her.

She swung open the door and stood there a moment, startled. Pearce was up. He'd harnessed Fritz, but he hadn't put on his shirt or sweater yet, although he'd donned his dark glasses once more.

He stood beside the bed, stretching like a large, sleek cat, flexing his arms and yawning.

"Oh," Mollie said, unused to the sight of so much bare and muscular male flesh. Maybe he didn't know she was there. She cleared her throat self-consciously. "Good morning," she said.

He grimaced and stretched more sinuously. "There's no such thing as a good morning. I've never understood putting those two words together."

She cocked one of her auburn eyebrows and tried to ignore the play of his muscles in the morning light. She went to put away her blankets and pillows. "One of those, eh?" she said. "A morning grouch."

"A devout morning grouch," he corrected, yawning again. "I'm glad to find you didn't fly the coop."

"I have nowhere to fly, remember?" she said, folding a blue blanket. "I'll find a place today."

He stopped stretching. He put his hands on his lean hips and frowned. "I thought you were going to—you know—help me."

"I will," she said, trying to sound as businesslike as possible as she folded the second blanket. "But that doesn't mean I have to stay with you. I can get a place close by. Pick you up in the morning. Drop you off at night."

He stood still for a long moment, the corner of his mouth turning down. His hair had fallen over his brow like a forelock. He pushed it back, the motion charged with the impatience of a man who hated mornings.

"Let's talk about it after coffee," he said at last. He reached for his shirt, groped before he found it, then signaled Fritz to lead him toward the bathroom.

"Do you want me to order coffee from room service?" Mollie asked in the same businesslike tone, plumping the pillow.

He stopped by the bathroom door, barely missing running into it. Mollie caught her breath. Somehow, he seemed less sure of himself than he had yesterday.

"This is New Orleans," he said, his tone mocking. "I don't want room service coffee. We'll go out for the real stuff. But you can phone the desk and see if they'll send up a couple of toothbrushes and a razor and some shaving cream and stuff. Damn! Where's the doorknob on this thing?''

He made his way inside and Mollie heard him bump into something and swear again. How odd, she thought. He seemed much more vulnerable today. She shrugged and dialed room service. She blessed whoever had invented it when a cheerful southern voice assured her that the hotel would gladly supply the missing necessities.

She hung up, realizing a luxury hotel certainly had its amenities. Being in a compromising situation wasn't *all* bad, Mollie thought ruefully, and almost laughed at her own predicament.

"DO I NEED TO TAKE your arm?" she asked as they left the room. "The sidewalk's going to be icy. Fritz may not be able to tell where it could be dangerous."

Pearce, obviously still not happy that it was morning, paused and considered. He seemed to think about the matter an inordinately long time. His face was grim, and finally he shrugged.

She linked her arm through his. "Stairs, straight ahead, about five paces," she said.

They descended to the hotel lobby, where Mollie once again felt overawed by the opulence. Everything seemed as stately and lush by daylight as it had the night before.

When they stepped outside, she gasped and Pearce swore under his breath as the wind hit them. It bit into flesh like a razor, its damp chill slicing to the bone. Even Fritz shuddered, as if he was trying to burrow more deeply into his fur.

Although Mollie was frozen, she looked around her in wonder. Flanking either side of the ancient brick streets were the famous quaint buildings of the French Quarter.

The fancy ironwork decorating their porches and balconies made them look as if they were edged in black lace.

Many of the balconies had Christmas lights woven through them, and Mollie could imagine how beautifully they must twinkle by night. Other balconies were adorned with huge red bows, garlands of pine branches, holly wreaths and decorated Christmas trees.

Hanging above the streets were strings of even more ornate decorations, which bobbed in the wind. A mule-drawn carriage went clattering by, its driver bundled up in a scarlet coat. The mule itself wore a wide-brimmed straw hat covered with poinsettias and holly sprigs, and two vases full of artificial Christmas flowers were somehow strapped to its harness. The breath of both mule and driver rose in frosty clouds.

"It's true," Mollie said, unconsciously huddling closer to Pearce for warmth. "We're in New Orleans."

"Yeah—and it's three times colder than New York," he grumbled. "Come on. To Jackson Square. We want the Café du Monde. West. Let's not just stand here, okay?"

"Sorry," Mollie said, trying to pull herself back to the job at hand. "Right and straight ahead. It's just...so wonderful."

She felt suddenly guilty that he couldn't see the wonders around them. She stayed close at his side, trying to watch for the worst patches of ice so that she could guide him around them. "I mean—it's great," she said. Briefly she allowed her attention to be caught by a fantastic display of Mardi Gras masks in a store window. "Do you want me to tell you what I see?"

Pearce, his face set against the cold, shrugged and tried to huddle more deeply into his light jacket. "If it makes you happy," he said without enthusiasm.

So Mollie steered and gawked and chattered as they made their way down the frosted sidewalk. "There's a courtyard with a fountain," she said. "It's a black fountain, with three tiers, but the water's all frozen—in a cascade—just like an ice sculpture."

"I'm going to be frozen like an ice sculpture if this keeps up," he muttered. "Is there a cab around? A dogsled? Four penguins with a sedan chair?"

Mollie laughed, but kept on describing things as vividly as she could. He kept complaining, but always in a way designed to make her laugh. It became a game that helped distract her from the cold.

"There's a courtyard with a sad-looking, frozen tree, all drooping and broken. It has big leaves, but they're all withered. I think it's a banana tree—and its bananas are all black and ruined."

"This weather'd freeze anybody's bananas," he snorted. "And their mangos."

"Oh," Mollie said sadly, looking at a low stone wall. A tiny gray shape lay there, stiff and lifeless. "There's a little lizard that died, Pearce. I think it's a chameleon. Not two inches long. How sad. It must have frozen to death."

He squeezed her arm. "Don't be sad. It's gone to lizard heaven."

She had to smile. "And what," she teased him, "is lizard heaven?"

"Oddly enough," he said with a shudder of cold, "it's exactly the same place as fly hell. All day long the lizards sit around in the sun, their tongues going 'thwip, thwip, thwip,' eating flies."

"But what happens to good flies?" she asked, laughing. "Don't they have a heaven?"

"I maintain that good flies, like good mornings, are a contradiction in terms. There are no good flies. But if we get to heaven, we can check."

At last they reached the Café du Monde, a low-slung beige building with green-and-white striped awnings at its arched entrances and windows. Although spindly little wire tables and chairs were set outside to serve as a sidewalk cafe, no diners were hardy enough to brave the cold today.

Inside, however, the place was crowded, despite the frigid weather. The fragrance of freshly fried doughnuts and rich coffee filled the air, making Mollie's stomach contract in hungry anticipation. They sat at one of the small tables, and Fritz settled down beside Pearce's chair gratefully, still shivering from his long walk. His eyes were half-shut, as if to close out the memory of the cold.

Mollie sat facing Pearce, who ordered for them. A rather harried waiter brought them steaming cups of café au lait and the crisp, aromatic little French doughnuts called *beignets*.

She set Pearce's coffee cup by his hand so he could find it easily and nudged his plate of *beignets* next to him. The coffee was delicious, strong, creamy and sweet, and she drank it gratefully.

Pearce had cut himself shaving, she noticed, a thin, inch-long slash across his chin. Once, on the way to the café, he had bumped his head badly on an awning, and once he'd misjudged the height of a curb and stumbled, his body leaning hard against hers for a moment.

Now he sat warming his hands around his white coffee mug. His jokes had stopped, and she missed them.

"So tell me," he said casually. "Tell me about the boyfriend. I suppose it was a boyfriend. What did he do?"

The question, so quiet, so lazy-sounding, startled her. She realized he was too perceptive for her to lie. She was an actress, but she felt somehow this man could read every nuance of her voice and he wouldn't be fooled by her acting, no matter how skillful.

She shrugged. "He didn't do much of anything. He lied."

Pearce didn't move. His hands stayed clamped around his coffee mug, but a muscle twitched in his cheek. "I see." He corrected himself irritably, "I mean, of course, I don't see, but I understand. What did he lie about?"

"Everything," she said. She managed to keep her voice from choking, but just barely. She wondered if Pearce had noticed.

He said nothing for a long moment. He appeared deep in thought, atypically serious. At last he spoke. "If he was a liar, why do you miss him?"

The question took her aback temporarily. He was right. Why had she mourned for a man who had never been honest with her?

"I don't miss him," she said slowly. "I miss what I thought he was. I thought he was...truthful. I thought he was ambitious. I thought he was brave." She paused, then decided to say it and be done with it. "And I thought he loved me. I was wrong about it all."

He picked up his coffee mug, put it to his lips and drank. He put the cup back down. He said nothing.

Mollie cocked her head philosophically. "So what? So it's over. Life goes on. And so do I."

He nodded. "Yes. You certainly do." His voice resonated with irony.

"And so," she went on, "does the business of the day. What is the business of the day? I need to find a room, but then I'll take you wherever you want to go."

She tasted her *beignet*. It was covered with so much powdered sugar she dared not breathe as she bit into it, for a cloud of white would have wafted from it. But the sweetness was delicious, even though she knew sugar had whitened her lips and chin. She wiped it away with a napkin.

She glanced at the people at the surrounding tables. Most of them were having *beignets,* too, and most of them bore the evidence—fine white sugar powdering their chests, chins, mouths. More than one diner had a sugary mustache, and all their tabletops were grainy with spills.

"Would you?" Pearce asked, and she heard suggestive challenge in his voice.

She looked at him again. His familiar sardonic smile played at the corners of his mouth, and one of his eyebrows lifted in a gesture that was serious and skeptical at the same time.

"Would I what?" she asked, not understanding the strange mix of emotions in his expression.

"Would you really take me wherever I want to go?"

She stared down into her coffee mug, suddenly realizing that the words smouldered with more meaning than she had intended.

"Within reason," she said, not looking at him. "There are certain points past which I don't intend to go."

He reached across the table. "Give me your hand."

She stared at his hand, lean, brown, strong and inviting. Without knowing why, wanting to and not wanting to, she gave him her own. His fingers tightened securely around hers.

"You're good company, Mollie," he said, his voice soft, low and persuasive. "I don't want you too far away. I'll rent a suite. You can have one set of rooms. I'll take the other. The door between us stays locked. That I promise. As long as you want it locked, it's locked."

She shook her head. "No," she protested. "I can't do that." But somehow she couldn't withdraw her hand. She was holding onto him almost as tightly as he held onto her.

"Mollie," he said, his voice suddenly taut. "Just stay by me. That's all I ask."

What's happening between us? Mollie thought in dismay, looking down at their tightly joined hands. Her knuckles had become dusted with powdered sugar and so had his. That should have made their gesture seem slightly absurd to her, but it did not.

It was as if the Café du Monde, with its pale stucco, its green-and-white stripes, its garlands and crowds and fragrances, had faded away into a fog, leaving only her and Pearce so strangely linked together.

Although one corner of her mind warned her sharply against this man, she ignored it. She would stay by him. She knew she would. It was as if she couldn't help herself.

CHAPTER FIVE

IT WAS HARD TO BELIEVE, Mollie told herself, yet somehow the three of them—she, Pearce and the serious, elderly dog—had become a team. In spite of the cold, Pearce wanted to walk, and walk they did.

They walked the French Market, which was a symphony of colors and smells. Sheltered, it was warmer than the street, full of tangy, mingling scents and fruits and vegetables that blazed with bright hues.

There were apples, oranges, lemons, limes, and grapes of pale green, deep red and rich purple. There were bins of green and yellow peppers, strings of crimson hot peppers and ropes of snowy garlics. Everywhere was color: bags of golden onions, heaps of grapefruits as yellow as suns, and mounds of pale green cabbages and blue-black eggplants.

A host of vendors of items other than produce crowded the market stalls as well. People were selling everything from T-shirts to turquoise jewelry and the sequined and feathered masks that seemed to be the trademark of New Orleans.

She and Pearce and Fritz walked Jackson Square, with its tall palm trees shivering in the chilly wind. Mollie tried hard to describe how dramatic the park's statue was: a giant figure of the lean General Andrew Jackson on his rearing horse, its forelegs pawing the wintry air. Both the general and his horse were glazed with frost.

As the morning wore on, more tourists ventured out to face the cold, and the street entertainers emerged to ply their trade in spite of the bitter weather.

A pair of jugglers tossed flaming torches back and forth. A black man dressed as Santa Claus played jazz on a saxophone. Another black man, thin and handsome, sat bundled up in front of three chessboards, offering to play three opponents at once. A girl in a top hat and spangles impersonated a robot dancing.

Up and down the length of Bourbon Street Pearce and Mollie and Fritz wandered, past the myriad of restaurants, bars, shops and galleries. A young man standing before the Believe It Or Not museum was eating fire as casually as another man might eat a candy bar.

They passed a voodoo museum, as well, and Mollie shuddered. There was something about New Orleans that made her believe that magic, both good and evil, could be real.

Once more she was struck by how much less certainly Pearce seemed to move today than yesterday. His movements were slower and sometimes awkward. He stumbled more than once, but he always caught himself and laughed.

Of all the wonderful sights and sounds of the French Quarter, Mollie thought the thing she would remember best would be Pearce's laughter and her own. There seemed to be nothing he couldn't turn into an irreverent joke if he chose to.

She tried to describe everything to him as clearly as possible, and he, in turn, kept up a running satiric commentary. She found that for the first time in months, she was having fun. It was a delicious feeling, intoxicating. It was like coming back to life.

Pearce said that to be good tourists, they had to have lunch at the Central Street Grocery, a crowded little hole-in-the-wall grocery store that repeatedly won top awards for serving the city's best sandwiches.

They sat at the counter, perched on stools, Fritz resting at their feet. They had the locally brewed beer, Dixie, and shared one of the store's famous mufallata sandwiches.

Mollie had thought nothing could be more delicious than breakfast at the Café du Monde, but now, tasting the mufallata, she was no longer sure. The sandwich was a tangy concoction of meats and cheese with an olive salad garnish on Italian bread. Every bite made her mouth tingle with delight.

"I'm never going back to New York," she said blissfully. "I'm going to stay here at this counter for the rest of my life and eat."

"You haven't tasted anything yet," Pearce teased. "New Orleans is a city of feasts."

Mollie gave a sigh of satisfaction, for the city did seem a feast for all the senses. Outside there was music in the streets and more music spilling from the doorways of the clubs, even though it was only noon.

Everywhere there were restaurants, and the scents of exotic cooking mingled with those of pine decorations and the dampness from the river. What must it be like, she wondered, when it was all bathed in warmth and sunshine? It must be paradise.

Even the inside of the little store was a banquet of sights, smells and tastes. The aroma of cheeses and spicy sausages filled the air, and the shelves were crowded with the jewel-like colors of containers, especially the green and scarlet tins and golden bottles of olive oil.

Suddenly, as happy as she was, she felt a wave of sadness that Pearce couldn't see all the color and character of the city.

"You haven't always been blind, have you?" she asked. She could tell that he must have been able to see once from the way he talked and how readily he understood her descriptions.

The crooked smile on his face died. "No," he said, his voice flat. He fingered the shaving cut on his chin.

"How long has it been?" she asked.

He lifted one shoulder in a careless shrug. "Not that long, actually."

"Oh." She frowned slightly. His answer was too vague to have meaning. "Do you want to tell me what happened?" She studied his profile. He had become suddenly solemn, distant. When he wasn't smiling, he seemed to have a different face altogether—serious, almost moody.

He toyed with the bottle of Dixie beer, the set of his mouth grim. "I'd rather not talk about it."

"Oh," she said again. She felt awkward, for she had blundered into a topic he found painful. She struggled to change the course of the conversation.

"What exactly do you do, anyway?" she asked. "You said something about entertainment."

One of his eyebrows arched more pointedly. He set down the beer bottle with a sharp report. "I'm . . . independently employed now. I used to work with a film company."

"Film company?" she asked, more puzzled than before. In what capacity could a blind man work for a film company? But then she thought perhaps she understood. Sometimes the loss of one sense sharpened others; perhaps that was why there were so many talented blind musicians. "Are you connected with sound? With recording and things?"

"Among other things," he said with the same maddening vagueness. He cocked his head with impatience. "Look, I'm just starting out on my own. My own projects. I don't like talking about that yet, either. You know."

She stared at him, nibbling her lower lip thoughtfully. Why was he so evasive? She knew of certain people, artistic types, who didn't like to talk about their work in progress. They thought it dissipated creative energy. But even their answers weren't as shadowy as Pearce's.

Was he hiding something? Somehow he did not seem the type. He was far too high-spirited and bold for secrets; they would be foreign to his nature.

"Let's not talk about me," he said, pushing the bottle away irritably. "Let's talk about you. You've got a great voice. Ever do voice-over work? Or think about doing voices for animation?"

He had caught her off guard, as he so frequently did. Mollie crumpled up her napkin, looking rueful. "I'm trying it when I get back to New York. For a series of educational videos, partly animated. I'm the voice of a germ."

He threw his head back and laughed.

Mollie drew herself up with all the dignity she could manage. "I plan to be the best germ I can be," she said. "You know the saying—'There are no small parts, only small actors.'"

"Usually said by someone assigning a small part," he answered. "I know some people who work in animation. They'd like you. Would you be interested?"

"I'm always interested in work," she said. "As long as it's honest."

The smile that had begun to hover again at the corner of his mouth disappeared. "Honest," he muttered. "You're always talking about honesty. Is it that important to you?"

"It's the most important thing in the world," she said with feeling.

"Because of the boyfriend?" There was sarcasm in his voice, almost a taunt.

"Partly." Mollie bit the word off. Michael's lies had been treacherous, painful and cowardly, and they had made her hate dishonesty with all her heart. Her parents had always taught her to tell the truth, and she had tried to do so. She had no use for people who didn't.

Pearce rested his elbow on the counter and his chin on his fist. She could see herself reflected in the black lenses of his glasses. "And what," he asked with elaborate casualness, "would you do if you found out that somebody else was doing the same thing? As your boyfriend? That somebody was lying to you? Even if he had good reason?"

"There's *no* good reason," she said with bitter conviction. "I'd turn my back on him and never speak to him again. I'd consider him the lowest of the low."

He reflected on this a moment, then nodded derisively. "A woman of principle. But that's impractical. Life isn't always that simple. You need work. What if this person had work for you?"

Mollie blinked in surprise. Money, of course, was something about which she always had to worry. "That person could talk to my agent," she said after a moment. "Right now I take work where I can get it. I have to. But that doesn't mean I have to respect the person I work for. Or even like him. Why?"

"No reason," he said smoothly. He reached for Fritz's harness. "Come on. Let's hit the bricks. I want to soak up all the atmosphere I can while I'm here."

Troubled, Mollie took his arm as he made his way through the grocery store's narrow aisles. She could feel the play of his bunched muscles even through his jacket and sweater. In the confines of the little store he seemed taller, more charged with power than ever.

But he stumbled slightly against an enormous can of olive oil jutting out into the aisle. He swore softly, tightened his hold on Mollie's arm and laughed mockingly at himself.

He's always laughing at everything, Mollie thought in perplexity. Had he been laughing at her for hating lies? It almost seemed so, but she wasn't sure. For a moment he had seemed, unlikely as it was, almost troubled.

Outside in the street a magician in a set of earmuffs and a rather ragged black cloak was doing complicated tricks with a knotted length of colored scarves. Like a tattered rainbow, the band of scarves floated through the air.

"Now you see it," the magician said with a wicked, flashing grin as it vanished. "Now you don't."

"Right," Pearce said cryptically.

LONG BEFORE LUNCH, Pearce had decided that not to see in New Orleans was almost more deprivation than he, a highly visual man, could stand.

But he was learning to understand how the mole would move, and to an animator movement was everything. It was key to the illusion of life. He could feel in his bones now what Moncrief Mole's pace would be, how he would carry himself, what obstacles he would encounter, how he would react. But it was hellish to him. He wondered how his uncle, Faron, had stood it with such good cheer all those years.

Today Pearce had opened his eyes only twice, both times to see the girl. The image of her was now imprinted on his brain, hovering there like a vivid picture from a dream that wouldn't go away.

The first time he had looked at her was in the morning, when she'd come back into the room from the bathroom. He'd vowed not to get involved with her, but when he heard her crying softly in the bathroom, the sound had done something to the pit of his stomach.

When she came through the door, he had wanted to see her face, to make sure she was all right. It gave his insides another peculiar wrench that she had looked both vulnerable and yet determined to be strong.

It had occurred to him at that moment how much he liked her face. It wasn't a classically beautiful face, not at all. But somehow her rounded cheekbones, her clear blue eyes, her generous mouth combined to give an incredible liveliness to her face, a fascinating vitality that made it torture to close his eyes again.

Then they had taken that long, cold walk to the Café du Monde, with her chattering and joking, forgetting her own problems so she could cope with his. He'd started playing verbal games with her, and she played back deftly, a natural at it. Her sense of humor was quick and cheerful, the perfect foil for his wilder, more acid one.

It had been depressingly cold, and voluntarily he had locked himself into a world of darkness, a world where he was prone to stumble and go astray, even with Fritz. But with her at his side, it hadn't really seemed depressing or cold or dark. Her presence was a kind of light, quietly stronger than any darkness he could impose.

He wasn't blind. He prized his sight and would do everything in his power to preserve it. But he had realized that if the darkness he stumbled through had been real, he would want someone like Mollie Randall by his side. Someone, in fact, exactly like Mollie Randall.

And so, in the Café du Monde, he had found himself breaking his own rule again when he'd held out his hand to her. He'd looked at her. She had that silly little knit hat that couldn't really keep her warm and that glorious cascade of hair almost crackling with fire in the morning light. Her searching look had pierced him through, giving him a lurching feeling, as if he were descending too quickly in an elevator.

He'd felt his blood quicken, his groin tighten, and when she put her hand in his, he got that lurching sensation again.

This is going to go away, he'd told himself. *I don't want this feeling, and it's going to go away.*

But it didn't go away. They walked and talked and laughed, and the feeling stayed.

He didn't like that. He didn't like it at all. He was a free man who intended to stay free.

THAT EVENING SHE SAT across from Pearce in a crowded, homey restaurant that specialized in Cajun food and haunting, yet fast-paced Cajun music. The walls were knotty pine, the tablecloths red-and-white checked, and a candle in an amber-colored glass sat on the tabletop, casting a warm, flickering light.

Pearce had been telling stories that Mollie found almost unbearably funny. "You didn't," Mollie begged. "Please—say you didn't." She had laughed until tears burned her eyes and blurred her vision. She had laughed until she literally hurt.

But Pearce had no mercy. "We did," he said with his crooked grin. They had both been talking about their childhoods. Because of her father, hers had sometimes been eccentric, but it seemed uneventful, even sedate compared to Pearce's.

"You were *devils,*" she laughed.

He shrugged. "So that was the third time the police came for us." He had been explaining how he and his brother, Harry, while in high school, had slipped into the city park one night. As a sort of war memorial, the park had a grounded jet fighter plane from the Korean War. Pearce and Harry had decided to build a fire in its nose cone and roast weenies. The police had arrived just when they were toasting marshmallows for dessert.

"How did you even *think* of such a thing?" Mollie demanded.

"I couldn't look at that jet and not think of it," he said, as if the answer were obvious. "I couldn't walk past that nose cone and not think, 'What a barbecue pit.'"

Mollie shook her head in a mixture of disapproval and amusement. The candlelight gleamed, making twin points of fire in his dark glasses. They had eaten a wonderful meal of red beans and rice spiced with a fiery sauce and complemented by squares of golden crumbly cornbread, soaked with butter.

She felt a warm glow of satisfaction, and she loved his stories. He was an excellent storyteller, and he and his brother sounded like boys out of some crazy, marvelous legend, each of their escapades outstripping the last.

"You must have been terrors," she mused.

"We were. We were close to being delinquents, I guess."

"Close?" Mollie teased.

He smiled, shrugged, and then his smile faded. "We came from a broken home. Our father left when we were little. Our mother couldn't...wasn't able to cope very well. I don't know. Maybe we did it for attention. Maybe to rebel. Maybe both. Anything For a Laugh—that was our motto."

She smiled sympathetically. She could clearly imagine him as he must have been, a tall boy with a careless grin and rebellious spirit, quick to laugh, yet with something of a loner's spirit in him. She wondered if he'd changed that much, if there was still a kind of loneliness in him, even better hidden now. "It's still your motto, isn't it?" she asked carefully. "Anything For a Laugh?"

He sipped his after-dinner drink. "More or less," he said with a slanting half smile.

"And what happened to Harry?" she asked, liking the way the candlelight gilded his regular features. He looked like a man cast from gold or bronze, with shadows dancing around the mysterious curve of his mouth. "Did he grow up to repent of his sins?"

All traces of humor vanished from Pearce's face. "No," he said, his voice expressionless. "Harry died. When he was seventeen. He was playing football and got hit, knocked out. The doctor said it was nothing. Next week he played again, got hit again. Only that time it killed him. It was a stupid, useless death, and my mother never got over it."

He kept his face blank, stony. She could tell that for all his devil-may-care attitude about most things, he hadn't gotten over it, either. The words, she sensed, had cost him, still pained him.

"Oh, Pearce," she said softly. "I'm sorry." She reached out and squeezed his hand. He caught her fingers and held them lightly. "What did you do?"

He caressed her knuckles, still not smiling. "For starters, I never touched a football again. I never even watched another game. I never want to hear one for the rest of my life." He shook his head, remembering. "The rest of it? I did what Harry and I had always done. I hid behind a lot of jokes. It was what Harry would have done if it had been the other way around. It was what Harry would have wanted."

Jokes, Mollie thought. *He's always buried the pain in laughter. No wonder he's so good at it.*

"And your mother?" she asked with concern.

He shrugged, shaking his head unhappily. "She never was very good at dealing with the world. She kind of lost any hold she had on reality after he died. I was fifteen. My Uncle Faron came and got us. Took us to live with him in Los Angeles." The smile touched the corners of his mouth again. "He couldn't do a lot with my mother, but he made me shape up. Did he ever. Wow."

He shook his head again, but this time he seemed ruefully amused by memories of his uncle.

Mollie's sympathies, always easily touched, made a knot of pain clench up in her throat, threatening to choke her. She drew her hand away from his because she liked the touch of it too much. She was beginning to like everything about Pearce Goddard too much. It was a disturbing sensation, both sweet and bitter at the same time.

"He must be a remarkable man, your Uncle Faron," she said. She let her hand fall into her lap, her fingers still tingling from his touch.

"He was," Pearce said, fondness in his voice. "He's gone now, too. That's why I was in New York. For his funeral. He'd moved back there a few years ago, after my mother died."

"Oh, dear, I *am* sorry," Mollie said, biting her lip. "Don't you have any family at all?"

His smile had a bitter twist. "My father's still alive—somewhere. I've got no interest in meeting him again. And I hear I have a couple of half sisters I've never met. But no, basically it's me. A lone wolf. And likely to remain so."

"Oh," Mollie said tonelessly. "You never got close to getting married—or anything?"

She immediately regretted the question. It was too personal. She watched his face closely for his reaction. Behind the dark glasses he almost seemed to wince, as if the memory pained or embarrassed him. But he flashed her a cynical grin. "Almost—once. By the skin of my teeth I escaped. I can't talk about it. It'd give me nightmares. Dance with me instead."

Mollie stared at him, her lips parted in astonishment. His mercurial changes always took her by surprise. "What?"

"Dance with me," he said. "Just because I don't want to marry a woman doesn't mean I don't like holding one. And I think I'd like to hold you. I know it, in fact."

She paused, trying to think sensibly. She wasn't sure she dared to be in his arms again; the feelings he awoke were too seductive, too difficult to resist. Besides, she had watched the people dancing to the Cajun music. It was like no dancing she had ever seen, full of complicated steps and twirls, with the movements of the hands almost as complex as those of the feet.

The cheerful wail of the fiddle and the melancholy voice of the concertina mingled their complex messages, and Mollie watched as the couples whirled in their intricate dance. "I can't dance like that," she said softly, by way of excuse. "I don't know if you ever saw how they dance, but—"

"We don't have to dance like they do," he said shortly. "We can dance any way we want, fast or slow, happy or sad. Who's to care but you and me?"

For the second time that day, he held out his hand to her. The music throbbed around them. She studied him for a long moment. The candlelight flickered and the dark glasses were like black pools in which she could lose herself. For the second time that day, she put her hand in his.

He stood. "Stay, Fritz," he said. Fritz sighed and laid his head back down on his paws. He seemed bone-weary, happy to rest as much as he could.

"Lead the way," Pearce said to Mollie. "And don't expect anything fancy. We'll be doing great if you still have ten toes when this is over."

His fingers, laced through Mollie's, tightened around hers possessively, and she found it had become laborious to draw her breath. It was as if his touch had tightened around her heart itself.

She led him to a corner of the dance floor that was almost deserted, barely lit. "Here," she said, turning to him. "This seems like a good place."

The exotic rhythms of the music pulsed through her body. Pearce reached out unerringly and put his arm around her waist, his strong fingers caressing the small of her back. Slowly he drew her to him.

He wasn't like Michael, she thought in confusion. He was far taller, more commanding, and he danced more closely, very closely, with her held tightly in his arms. She could feel the power of his thighs radiating against her, own the hardness of his chest so close that her breasts tingled at the intimacy of his touch.

"Put your arms around my neck," he said, bending his face so that his cheek pressed against hers. He hadn't shaved since morning, and the skin of his face was slightly raspy, like warm sandpaper, but Mollie didn't mind. His breath against her ear and neck tickled, and the harshness of his skin against the softness of hers was an exciting contrast.

She raised her arms and wound them around the firmness of his neck. He began to move, although they barely stirred from their corner of the floor. Their steps were not designed to take them anywhere, only to keep them near each other.

Mollie closed her eyes and leaned against Pearce's chest. They were doing what her mother and father had always called "slow dancing," which meant mostly standing with their arms around each other, swaying sensuously to the music.

The music's pace had picked up again, and around them she could hear the fast steps and occasional jubilant cries of the dancers. But she and Pearce moved together to a more primal beat. "Nobody else is dancing like this," she said softly against his shoulder.

"I told you," he said, his voice low. "It doesn't matter what anybody else does. We can dance any way we want." He ran his hand over her hair, smoothing it.

"People may think we're crazy," she murmured dreamily.

"People may be right." She felt his hands stroking her hair again, lacing his fingers through it, toying with it.

She squeezed her eyes shut more tightly. Was this what his world was like? she wondered. Darkness didn't seem frightening or formidable when she was in his arms. The world had shrunk to the size of the two of them, swaying in each other's arms to a music that was foreign, yet magical.

Pearce's original plans had called for them to move on to Preservation Hall to hear its famous jazz band. But somehow they never made it. As the night wore on, Pearce and Mollie spent it in each other's arms, dancing their own dance in a shadowy corner, the rest of the world forgotten. They spoke little, but to Mollie it hardly seemed to matter.

At midnight the band announced it would play its last song, "Louisiana Blues." Pearce drew her to him more tightly still and buried his face against the silken, fragrant cloud of her hair. She sighed happily and turned her face up to his.

He stopped dancing and so did she. Once more Pearce got the familiar lurching-in-the-elevator feeling. He put his hands on either side of her face, reveling once more in the feel of her thick hair, the smoothness of her skin. He found himself, almost without volition, lowering his mouth to hers and kissing her, a long and searching kiss, there in the privacy of their corner.

He was going to have to tell her the truth, he thought. Somehow, someway, he was going to have to tell her the truth as soon as possible. Tonight. He couldn't go on with this charade any longer.

PEARCE WAS ATYPICALLY silent as they walked back to the hotel, Mollie noticed worriedly. Perhaps it was because the iron hand of the cold had closed down around the city again, driving most people inside and gripping the French Quarter in an unnatural quiet. The Christmas lights in the building's lacy grillwork twinkled and winked, making the nearly deserted Bourbon Street look not merely festive with Christmas, but enchanted.

There were only a few other people on the street and Fritz limped tiredly down the icy sidewalk. Perhaps that was what Pearce was worried about, Mollie thought. The old dog had done well all day, but when they'd arrived at the Cajun restaurant, the dog had almost collapsed, grateful to do nothing more strenuous than sleep.

Or, she wondered, was something deeper troubling Pearce? She was, in truth, troubled herself. They had danced like two people falling in love, but that, she knew, was impossible.

She was still getting over Michael—heaven only knew how long it would take to get over him completely, if she ever did. She couldn't possibly be falling in love with another man. That would be self-deception; trying to escape into a new relationship on the rebound from an old one. She must, she warned herself, be careful.

More than one woman had leaped into a disastrous relationship to soothe the pain of a love affair gone wrong. She had seen it happen dozens of times in college and marveled at how silly such women were. But now she was acting precisely the same way herself. It was insane.

Besides, she told herself, trying to be sensible, Pearce was a free spirit, determined not to be tied down by anything or anyone. He'd made that abundantly clear. It was one of the few things about himself that he *had* made clear.

No, they were going to be together only a few days. She mustn't forget that; they would have to part. They lived on opposite coasts, a continent apart. Whatever his business was, he said he had just gone independent. His energies would be spent in his work. And hers would be spent trying to stay brave in the world that had so frightened Michael, the world of acting.

When they reached the hotel, Pearce tried to get adjoining suites for them, but the hotel had none available. The cold spell was creating havoc in the city's accommodations. All over the French Quarter pipes were bursting, ceilings leaking, furnaces breaking down, and rooms were being closed off, unrentable and unrented. This hotel, for all its luxuries, was no different. The entire east wing was without heat.

"Stay in the room we had," Pearce told Mollie at last. "I can get another one down the hall."

She agreed mutely. She still felt uncomfortable about taking his charity, although he insisted it wasn't charity and she was more than earning her keep. They walked upstairs in mutual silence, the dog hobbling.

"You're awfully quiet," Pearce said when she took his key from him and unlocked the door to his new room.

"I was thinking the same thing about you," she said rather wanly. "I'll come in and show you where everything is."

She was further dismayed to see the room he had taken was smaller and far less comfortable than the one he had given her. "You can't do this," she protested. "Why should I live like a queen while you go without?"

Pearce's handsomely boned face grimaced slightly, as if the matter weren't worth discussing. "They're starting to have heating problems on this side of the hall, too. You were out in the cold with me most of the day. I hope you'll be with me tomorrow. At least you can sleep warmly tonight."

Oh, heavens, Mollie thought in consternation, it all got more confusing than ever when he was kind. Was ever a man such a combination of gentleman and rascal as Pearce Goddard?

"I can't—" she began.

He cut her off. "You have to. It's the way I want it. It's the way we'll do it."

She sighed and looked down at Fritz, who was already curled up in exhausted sleep, snoring wearily on a small throw rug.

"Look," Pearce said, his voice kind again. "Go hang up your coat and freshen up. I'll order us a couple of brandies. Then come back. We have to talk."

"Talk?" Mollie said. An ugly suspicion raised itself in her mind, like a reptile rearing up. Had all his charm and warmth and gentleness tonight been just a sly way of making her eager for his bed? And, after the way they had danced, wasn't it likely that he'd think she'd want to sleep with him?

She laughed nervously. "We can talk tomorrow."

"I'd rather do it now," he said, unsmiling. "While I'm in the mood. It's important."

"I—" She saw the frown lines between his eyes, knew he was serious. But about what was he so enigmatically serious? Just because they had danced and kissed didn't mean she was willing to make love to him. She realized once more, with a frisson of uneasiness, just how little she knew about him.

"Listen," she said. "It's late. I'm still not sure about this—this staying so close to each other. It's a strange situation."

He took a step toward her, a purposeful step. She took one backward, in the direction of the door. "I'm going to my room," she said.

The dark glasses covering his eyes were like disks of black mystery, and she was not any better at guessing what they hid. Tenderness? Lust? Scheming? Sincerity? After their long, strangely playful day together, it had been too easy to melt into his arms, to forget the rest of the world, forget tomorrow. It would be easy to do it again; tempting to do it with more passion.

But the rest of the world did exist, Mollie told herself, no matter what a person wanted to pretend in moments of desire. And tomorrows always came, demanding their debts, bringing their consequences, extorting their payments.

She looked at Pearce's powerful body, which gave off an aura of coiled energy. She looked at his face, which was more intent than she'd ever seen it. If she stayed any longer, he would kiss her again. She knew.

She took a deep breath and made her decision. "I'm going to my room," she repeated firmly. She turned and left, not allowing herself to look behind when she heard his voice.

"Are you coming back?" he asked. His tone was curt, demanding.

She hurried down the hall toward her own door. "I don't know." She shook her head, gazing down at the hall's scarlet carpet.

"I'll order the brandies. I'll phone you," he said, determination in his voice. "Mollie? We have to talk. Trust me."

She opened her door and slipped inside, locking it behind her. Trust him, he had said. If only she could. How could she trust him when she no longer trusted herself?

She shed her coat and hung it up. She had felt no doubts or fears about him in the restaurant, when they had been wrapped in a magic cocoon of music. She had clung to him and he to her. She had even, she remembered, trusted him in her long, involved, stressful dreams of the night before.

He would call her soon, she knew, asking her to come to him again. He had said doors between them would stay locked unless she wanted it otherwise. Did she want it otherwise?

She had never spent a day so unexpected and enchanted as this one. So many new sights, such wonderful sounds and delicious tastes, so much laughter, and all of it touched by the mystery of Pearce. Who was he, really, and what did he want from her? She wondered, even, what she really wanted from him—perhaps nothing more than comfort. No, she couldn't believe that.

What would she tell him when he called?

The phone rang.

Decide, its harsh cry said. *Decide.*

CHAPTER SIX

Mollie's heart beat so swiftly it seemed to go *tick, tick, tick*.

She picked up the receiver. "Hello?" She kept her husky voice under perfect control.

There were three throbbing seconds of silence.

A woman's suspicious voice came vibrating through the wire. "Who *is* this?" it snapped.

"Mollie Randall," Mollie said, surprised.

"Is this room 242? Did they connect me with the right room?"

"This is room 242." Mollie frowned slightly, not understanding what the problem was.

"And just *who* did you say this was?" the woman's voice demanded. Its tone was icily angry.

"Mollie Randall," Mollie repeated.

"Well, Mollie Randall," the woman said with exaggerated false sweetness, "just where did he pick *you* up? I thought he was going to be there with that little tart from Tampa—Melissa."

Mollie's face went stiff from shock. With a wave of dismay she realized that this woman was calling for Pearce, and she sounded not only angry, but extremely possessive. Mollie said nothing in her own defense, for at the moment she could think of nothing to say. Pearce had indeed picked her up, although she had done nothing wrong—yet.

"Ha," said the woman, a sneer in her voice. "Just as I thought. He's there, isn't he? Let me talk to him. This instant."

"He isn't here," Mollie replied defensively, coming back to herself. And, because the woman's unwarranted remarks had offended her, she plunged into the fray, ready to ask questions of her own. "Who is this? And what do you want?"

"I *happen* to be the woman he was supposed to marry last week," the woman said coldly. "Not that it's any of *your* business. He and I have a few things to settle. And you, my dear, can start packing. The man is *taken*. By *me*. Let me talk to him. Right now."

At the woman's words, Mollie's blood chilled so much it seemed to congeal. *Married?* Pearce was supposed to have been married this holiday? And like Michael—cowardly, lying Michael—he had found someone else instead? Melissa—the "friend" who couldn't make it from Tampa.

"He isn't here," Mollie repeated through clenched teeth.

"I know he's there," the woman insisted nastily. "Harry told me everything. So put him on."

Harry? Mollie thought, half-sick. Had Pearce even lied about that, about his own brother being dead? The whole story about Harry's death must have been nothing but a cheap fabrication, designed to win her sympathies. Well, she thought darkly, it had worked, hadn't it?

"He isn't here," Mollie said for the third time, her voice as steely as the edge of a sword. "Try room 247. And don't try to insult me anymore. I won't take it."

She hung up the phone with a resounding crash. Nausea swirled within her, born of anger more intense than she had ever known. Tossing her hair, she began to pace across the room's blue carpet.

What sort of man was Pearce? she asked herself, folding her arms across her chest. It was an unconscious gesture, performed as if it could both physically contain her fury and protect her heart, which felt so numb it might be dead.

She locked her teeth together, her jaw tensed and her eyes narrowed. She snatched a pillow off the bed and threw it across the room as hard as she could. It bounced cheerily off the blue striped silk wallpaper.

Oh, she thought in anger and disgust, crossing her arms again, how could she have been so stupid twice in a row? She had done it again, gotten involved with another man exactly like Michael, who didn't have an honest bone in his body.

How *charming* Pearce had been, what a delightful *companion* he had been, Mollie thought, fuming with resentment. How *gentle* he could pretend to be in all his power, how *sensitive* he hinted he could be, under his beguiling devil-may-care surface.

She had been moved almost to tears by the story of his dead brother, and she had pitied him because he had no family. They were probably all alive and in the very pink of health—from Harry to his mother and his Uncle Faron. They were probably all as healthy and lively as a tribe of circus acrobats, despite his killing them off regularly whenever he wanted to woo yet another naive and gullible woman.

Was he compensating for his blindness by collecting as many women as he could? He was probably trying to prove how much of a man he was, even if he couldn't see.

Like Michael, Pearce had promised to marry one woman, then had betrayed her, Mollie thought in fury.

He had betrayed her to make a carefree assignation with a second woman—Melissa, the so-called "tart from Tampa."

When Melissa was delayed by the bad weather, he lost no time. He quickly found a third woman, smoothly luring Mollie into his life and almost into his bed.

Of course he was charming, she thought bitterly. A seducer couldn't seduce if he wasn't charming, could he? Of course he was fascinating and exciting and provocative. That was his act, his bait in the cat-and-mouse game of sex.

Maybe charm and sex were even his business, she thought with harsh suspicion. Maybe that was why he was so vague about his profession: he was nothing better than a gigolo. He seduced women for money, or if they had no money he seduced them for the fun of it, and Mollie must have simply been enormous fun for him because she was so reluctant to become involved—

The phone rang again, cutting into her venomous chain of thought. She picked up the receiver angrily. If it was the woman calling to berate her once more, Mollie would hang up on her again, more loudly than before. Mollie hadn't called Michael's girlfriend to upbraid her, and she wasn't about to take any such treatment herself.

This time, however, the voice was Pearce's. It was low and tense. "Mollie," he said, "there's been a misunderstanding."

"Yes," Mollie said, more frost in her voice than in the frigid air outside. "There certainly has."

"That woman isn't my fiancée. Come down to my room. The brandies are here. I'll explain. I was a fool ever to get involved with her. I broke it off—"

"Break off this conversation, too," Mollie ordered. "I'm not coming to your room, you—you lothario."

"I'm not a lothario," he answered. "I'm a red-blooded male, *genus Americanus,* who broke up with one woman because she was too damned jealous—"

"Jealous with reason," Mollie retorted. "You came down here to be with a second woman. Your fiancée wasn't happy to find you'd already progressed to a third."

"Mollie," he said, a dangerous evenness in his tone, "I told you I was meeting a friend from Tampa. What did you think? I'm an adult, I don't have any commitments to anybody but myself, and if I wanted to meet a woman and spend the holidays with her, that's my privilege. She couldn't make it and I met you instead—"

"Listen," Mollie said hotly, "I don't like being taken for the 'other woman.' I know how painful it is to find out there *is* one. If you want to cry about all this on somebody's shoulder, I suggest you call up your brother Harry. And tell him, 'Welcome back to earth' from me."

"*What?*" His voice rumbled like indignant thunder.

"You heard me," she snapped back. "Your brother. Your—your girlfriend told me your brother Harry gave her this room number. Rising from the grave has apparently made him indiscreet. In short, he blabbed."

A moment of loaded silence pulsed between them. When he spoke, his voice was far icier than hers. "My brother Harry's been dead twenty-one years," he asserted. "There's more than one guy named Harry in the world. Harry Bidford's my neighbor, dammit. He's picking up my mail and feeding my fish while I'm gone. And what kind of hothead are you not even to give me a chance to explain? Good God, I thought you were a better woman than that."

Mollie's hand clenched around the phone so tightly that her fingers went as numb as her heart. She sat down heavily on the bed's satiny edge.

There had been such true disdain in his tone, such completely righteous resentment that she was taken aback. Had she angrily leaped to a false conclusion and insulted his brother's memory? If she had, it was a terrible thing to have done. She tried to sort through her tumbled thoughts. The woman had only said "Harry." She hadn't said anything about Harry being Pearce's brother.

"Listen," Pearce almost hissed in her ear. "I know she probably said abusive things to you. I know too well what she's capable of. But that's a side she never showed me until I said it was over. She played it sweet for a long time. So sweet it must have nearly killed her. But I couldn't spend the rest of my life with that woman. She was jealous of everything—my work, my ambitions, everything. Even my uncle."

Mollie listened, a blush of shame suffusing her face. Somehow Pearce's words rang with reason and truth. The woman had sounded jealous: clinging and overbearing and downright mean. She wanted to believe Pearce. But she was afraid to.

"I don't *have* to explain anything to you," he said, a shade of the old derision in his voice. "The only reason I will is that I like you. I like you a lot. The woman—her name's Irina Thomas. She comes from a very powerful family in Hollywood. We worked with each other. We drifted into a . . . relationship."

"You don't have to tell me," Mollie said, her emotions so conflicted that her jaw trembled. "I didn't ask for any explanation."

Her comment sounded cool and defensive, but in truth she was confused and more than a little abashed. She had been angry at him, because she thought he was being deceptive. But she had to admit she had also been jealous—just like the unpleasant Irina, but with far less right.

"No. I don't have to tell you. But I said I wanted to," he corrected. "All right. She wanted to get married, and I thought, what the hell? I'm thirty-six, we've got things in common, maybe it wouldn't be so bad. I was wrong. It was bad. It couldn't have been worse. We couldn't agree on anything. Then when my uncle got sick in November, she didn't want me to go to him. It might screw up her precious wedding plans. I loved this guy. I'm supposed to let him die alone because of this woman's stupid high society plans? All of a sudden, I thought, 'Lady, I've got to get on with my life. Go my own way.' I told her so. End of story."

Mollie said nothing in reply. She sat on the bed's edge, her teeth worrying her lower lip. Once more she found herself wanting to believe him. She didn't even understand why she wanted so badly, almost desperately, to believe him.

"Mollie?" His low voice made her shiver slightly. A tingling shudder ran up her spine, then down. "Are you listening?"

She tried to grip the phone less tightly. "Yes," she said, then bit her lip more sharply.

His voice took on a gentleness that for some reason made her shiver even harder. "If it makes you feel better, I won't ask you to come down here again tonight. If it makes you feel . . . less threatened. All right?"

She paused, once more ashamed of all the evil thoughts she'd entertained about him. He wasn't going to try to coax and beguile her into his bed. He was offering to keep his distance, play the gentleman.

"All right," she answered at last. She was grateful, relieved, yet at the same time filled with an odd feeling for which she could not find a name. It seemed a mixture of pain and yearning.

"Mollie," he said, and the intensity in his voice made her tremble as if the room's windows were open, with all the night's cold air pouring in. "We have to talk. We *have* to. Soon. There are…things I have to find a way to make you understand. But it needs to be the right time, the right place, the right mood. All right?"

"All right," she repeated, but she didn't understand. Once again she had the feeling that something was occurring between them, something totally improbable. Yet somehow, in his presence, even in the presence of his voice, the impossible sometimes seemed possible.

He was a man who made her feel as if the world could turn to magic at any moment. He could somehow make it seem as if some fabulous reality was about to come round the corner and say, "Ah, there you are, you two. I've been expecting you," and everything in her life would be changed, would be enchanted, and the enchantment would last forever.

"Mollie?" he asked again.

She hugged herself, wishing the way he said her name didn't affect her the insane way it did.

"Good night, Mollie," he said. "Sweet dreams, love."

She heard the click of his receiver settling into place. Unclenching her numbed fist, she set the receiver of her own phone back into its cradle.

Weary, confounded and emotionally drained, she lay down on the bed, curling up like an exhausted child. "Love," he had said. Love. Once, with Michael, she had thought she knew what the word meant. Now she was no longer sure.

She pulled the edge of the satin coverlet over her as Pearce had done to his half-naked body the night before. Although she was still clothed, her body tingled, shivering as it lay where his had lain.

No, she told herself, she was simply still cold. She was freezing, in fact. Had something else gone wrong with the hotel's heating system? she wondered. Was this side of the hall without heat now, as well?

Perhaps, she thought, the events of the night had frozen her more thoroughly than the outside cold. Perhaps too many intense and frightening feelings had sucked all the warmth from her blood, leaving her chilled throughout.

The coverlet didn't warm her. Hugging her arms around herself didn't warm her, either. She was afraid to admit that she could think of only one thing that could make her warm again—to lie in the arms of the mysterious, perplexing, dangerous man down the hall.

PEARCE LAY ON HIS BACK, hands behind his head, frowning at the ceiling. Fritz was still curled on the throw rug, snoring and wheezing, shuddering in his sleep. The room was freezing and the old dog was cold.

Swearing silently to himself, Pearce rose and stripped a blanket from his bed and tucked it around Fritz, who snorted and stirred but didn't awaken. He looked at the dog. The shepherd suddenly seemed ancient to him, worn out.

Pearce's dark glasses lay on the nightstand. Since Irina's call he hadn't bothered to pretend to be blind. He was too worried to care. He stroked Fritz's graying head and then lay down on the bed again, staring moodily at the ceiling. It had a crack in it shaped roughly like a question mark, and Pearce was not amused by the irony.

He had wanted to tell Mollie the truth; he had meant to tell her. Then Irina had butted in, like the evil fairy who ruins the party in the children's story, cursing events with her jealous spell.

That Irina had berated and insulted Mollie he was sure. That she had upset her was evident; Irina had seriously shaken Mollie's faith in him, and he could only hope he'd put it right. But this was no time, after all that had transpired, to shake it even more by admitting he could see.

Irina, he thought blackly. She was small and blond and beautiful in a petite, deceptively elfin way. Her father owned the controlling interest in TAS, Thomas Animation Studios, where Pearce had been director-in-chief. Irina was Russ Thomas's only child, and she always got what she wanted. She had decided that she wanted Pearce.

She almost got him, too, he thought, remembering ruefully. But her everlasting selfishness couldn't contain itself; it kept getting in the way. He had projects of his own he wanted to follow, most importantly the mole movie. She would have none of it. His job, when her father stepped down, would be to run TAS the way it had always been run, no changes, no innovations, nothing new.

He'd lose money with his stupid mole movie, she'd kept nagging. Why did he want to risk all that time and money when he could be a rich studio head? What he wanted to do was too ambitious, it was impossible, nobody could succeed at it—why couldn't he stick with what was tried and true?

He'd finally realized that she was actually jealous of the project; it would take too much attention away from her. A grown woman, he thought in disgust, jealous of a make-believe mole. Unbelievable. Sickening.

Their last and most spectacular clash had come when it became obvious that Faron, who had long been ill, was going to die. Irina's father said he couldn't spare Pearce; it was impossible to give him any time off. Irina said Faron was going to die anyway, and nothing Pearce could do would change that, so what did he think he was doing, trying to run off to New York and disturb all her carefully made plans?

Something in Pearce snapped. He'd told her father he was bloody well going to his uncle, and if that meant he lost his job, he lost his job. He told Irina there was no sense in their getting married when they obviously didn't want the same kind of life. If her father wanted to fire him over that, that was fine, too.

He'd gone to New York and been with Faron when he died. He'd had no idea of how much money Faron had quietly made in the last part of his life. Faron had bought a little stock here, a little stock there, and over the years the money had accumulated: a million and a half dollars of it.

"It's going to you," Faron had told him. "So you can start making that damn mole movie you've been talking about all these years."

Faron had looked frail and shrunken in his hospital bed, but he hadn't lost his sense of humor. "That mole is me, isn't he?" he demanded with a rasping chuckle.

Pearce had to admit that yes, the mole had been inspired by Faron, who had never allowed his blindness to interfere with his remarkable independence.

"Set in New Orleans, is it?" Faron asked, pleased.

Yes, Pearce said, it was. He would call it *Moncrief Mole Goes South*. In his dreams, he saw a series of features about the mole and the mysteries he solved: *Moncrief Mole Goes West*—to Wyoming, *Moncrief Mole Goes North*—to Alaska, *Moncrief Mole goes East*—to Tokyo.

"Ah," Faron sighed with satisfaction. "I loved New Orleans. So did Fritz. He loved the smells. All that food. He must have thought his nose had gone to heaven."

Pearce had smiled. He'd never thought of it that way. He supposed New Orleans was a banquet of scents to a dog.

"I want you to do some things for me," Faron said, feebly trying to shift his body in the bed. Pearce put his arm around the old man, helping ease him to a different position.

"First," Faron said, trying to force more strength into his voice, "get that movie made. Second, when I die, I don't want any mourning. I've had a good life, but it's worn me out, and I'm ready to go. So when you go home, flirt with the prettiest girl on the plane. Do that for me. And, finally, take care of Fritz. He's been a good and faithful servant. If you go to New Orleans, you might take him. Ah, how he loved the smells."

Pearce agreed, a painful knot in his throat. He'd squeezed his uncle's shoulder. "Consider it done," he said.

He'd stayed a week in New York after Faron died, straightening out the details of his estate. He'd called Irina's father, Russ Thomas, and said he wasn't coming back to TAS, that he was going his own way. Russ said he was a fool, but that it was just as well he was going—Irina didn't want him around TAS any longer. Irina had called, swearing at him and saying he couldn't be trusted. She never wanted to see him again, she said.

Fine, Pearce had said and meant it. He didn't know exactly how he'd hatched the scheme of pretending to be blind so that he could start getting into the character of the mole. He supposed it was a combination of things: he was finally starting on the film, and it took place in New Orleans, and he had to transport the dog. And Faron had said the dog loved New Orleans.

It had seemed a great idea, a liberating idea, full of high spirits and good fun. To make it better, he'd called Melissa, who was an airhead, but a sweet-natured, uncomplicated airhead whose main goal in life was to have as much fun as possible. She thought it would be "a hoot" guiding him around New Orleans. All she'd asked was to stay in the best hotel and eat in the best restaurants and that he buy her one of those pretty feathered masks, the really expensive ones.

Pearce stared at the question mark on the ceiling, the lines of his face rigid. It had seemed so simple and lighthearted and right. Faron, who had an extremely quirky sense of humor, would have loved it. But then there was the storm. And then there was Mollie.

Mollie, he thought, shaking his head back and forth on the pillow in unhappiness. He had to tell her the truth. But he had to keep her from walking away in disgust.

At first he'd told himself he'd wanted her around because he needed somebody, anybody, to guide him. He'd told himself it was her voice, that was all, that made her special. He needed her voice so he'd keep her around. He'd told himself a lot of things.

But the truth was that he wanted her for a lot more reasons than he'd admitted. He wanted her in all kinds of ways that he shouldn't, especially considering he was jobless and about to take a multimillion-dollar gamble.

It would take him at least three years of his life and more work than a sane person would even want to think about.

He was preparing to risk everything he had—money, career, reputation—and after Irina, he had no intention of asking anybody to share that risk with him. Hell, he had no *right* to ask anybody to share it.

But he didn't want to lose Mollie Randall. And when he told her the truth, he would probably lose her. Her voice and her freckles and her glorious red-gold hair and her laughter would be gone.

It shouldn't matter, he kept telling himself. It shouldn't matter. Besides, he had a job to do. He had to keep learning about the mole; who knew when he could afford to come to New Orleans again?

It was an impossible situation.

He lay awake half the night, thinking about Mollie and staring at the question mark.

MOLLIE STOOD BEFORE Pearce's door, steeled herself and knocked. She was going to make the best of things, she told herself. She wasn't going to let herself get more involved with him; she wasn't going to entertain the foolish idea that she might be falling in love with him.

"Your head should always rule your heart," her father always said. "When it can't, you'll either be in love or in big trouble. Unfortunately, the way the world works, you'll probably be in trouble. So be careful, kid."

She was determined to be careful. She already had enough trouble and needed to bring no more down upon herself. Raising her hand, she knocked again, a smart no-nonsense, businesslike rap.

She heard Pearce stumble against something, mutter, and at last swing the door open. She stared up into his black glasses. His face was drawn, the muscles in his jaw tense, as if he hadn't slept well. He hadn't shaved, and stubble shadowed the lower part of his face. It was the third day he'd worn the same clothes and they were starting to look crumpled.

"Are you all right?" she asked in concern.

"I'm fine," he said shortly. "It's Fritz. Something's wrong with him."

"Oh, *no!*" Her voice shook with dismay and her vow to stay unemotional and uninvolved was forgotten. She had been worried all along about Fritz. He was a gallant, dignified old dog and she dreaded anything happening to him.

Brushing past Pearce, she fell on her knees beside the throw rug. Fritz looked up at her with something akin to bewilderment in his beautiful amber eyes.

Seeing her beside him, the dog tried to rise, but his back legs wouldn't support his body weight. He swayed, made a sideways motion with his hindquarters that seemed involuntary, then sank helplessly back to the rug with a whimper that almost broke Mollie's heart.

"Oh, Fritz," she moaned, stroking his head. "Oh, poor Fritz." What if he was dying? she thought in panic. What would Pearce do then? And what about right now? Was the dog in pain or had he moaned because he was frightened? They had to take care of him.

Do something, she told herself. *Take charge. Do what has to be done. Be coolheaded. As Dad would be. As Mother would be.*

"We've got to get him to a vet," she said, holding Fritz's head in her lap and stroking him, trying to soothe him. "I'll look for one in the phone book."

"Mollie," Pearce said, still standing in the doorway. His hands were in his pockets and the set of his mouth was grim. "I told you last night that we had to have a talk—"

"Oh, not now," she said impatiently, looking down at the unhappy dog. Fritz gazed back at her. He seemed to look deeply into her eyes as if in supplication, and he whimpered again.

"It's important," Pearce said. His tone was flat, as if he'd willed all emotion out of it.

"I don't care," Mollie returned. She didn't care if he apologized about last night, or if he expected her to apologize. Such things seemed inconsequential. "We've got to take care of this first," she said with feeling. "He's suffering. I think he's scared half to death. He's trembling. And it's freezing in here. Oh, why didn't you take my room?"

She pulled the rumpled blanket back around the dog, tucking it beneath him tightly to keep him warmer.

"Mollie," Pearce said, his voice tight.

She couldn't face a serious discussion, not now, at a time like this. Fritz whimpered again.

"First things first," she said firmly and rose. "I mean it. I'm not interested in your personal life. I'm interested in helping Fritz."

She turned her back on Pearce, picked up the phone book and began flipping through it. She found the veterinary listing in the yellow pages, but she didn't know New Orleans well enough to tell where the offices were located.

Think clearly, she told herself. *Stop wasting time.* In exasperation she shut the book, picked up the phone and dialed the front desk.

"This is Miss Randall from room 242," she said briskly. "I'm calling for Mr. Goddard in room 247. We have an emergency here. His guide dog's sick." She took a deep breath, trying to marshall her thoughts. "I want you to do three things. First, call the closest veterinary and tell him that the dog can't seem to use its hind legs—and that he should expect us as soon as possible. This *is* an emergency. Next, call us a taxi to take us there. And last, send up a bellhop to 247 to carry the dog. We'll need him as soon as possible. Thank you."

She set the receiver back into the cradle and turned to look at Fritz. He was struggling to rise again. Once more he whimpered and collapsed.

"Oh," Mollie said, running her hand through her hair in despair, "this is terrible." Tears sprang to her eyes.

"You certainly took charge of things," Pearce said. She couldn't tell if his tone held admiration or irony or a mixture of both. "You're quite the little organizer in an emergency, aren't you?"

"I don't feel in charge," she said, going to the closet and getting his jacket. "Here." She thrust it into his hands.

He shrugged into the jacket. "You didn't have to ask for a bellboy to carry the dog," he said from between his teeth.

"He's too heavy for me to carry, and you shouldn't carry him," Mollie said, sinking to the floor to cradle the dog's head in her lap again. "Oh, poor Fritz. Don't worry. We're getting help."

"I'm perfectly capable of carrying my own dog," Pearce said. "Look, Mollie, I have to tell you—"

"You *shouldn't* carry him and that's that," she almost snapped, her voice quavering. "What if you fell down the stairs? If you don't care about yourself, what about him? You could hurt him worse than he is already."

"Oh, good Lord," Pearce said, disgust in his voice, "you're crying."

"So what?" she challenged, wiping away a tear. Another replaced it almost immediately. "It's not a crime."

"Mollie, don't cry," he said, shaking his head in frustration. "Please."

Fritz stared up at her soulfully. How gray his muzzle was, Mollie thought, biting her lip. How gray the patches of hair above his eyes. The dog, trying to rise again, started to stagger to his feet, even though it only meant he would fall again.

"No, Fritz, no," Mollie begged, gently pushing his hindquarters back down to the floor. "Lie down. Stay. That's a good boy." Her voice caught in a stifled sob.

"Mollie," Pearce said, his face more taut than before. "Don't cry, dammit." He paused, as if searching for a reason, any reason. "It—it upsets the dog."

"All right," Mollie said, wiping away another tear. She set her chin stubbornly. "I won't." But her voice, trained though it was, wobbled dangerously.

Pearce turned and leaned his forehead against the blue papered wall. He hit the wall dispiritedly with the flat of his fist. "My life is hell," he said.

He was terribly upset about the dog, Mollie thought. She would have to try to be braver, for his sake.

THE VETERINARY, Dr. Broussard, was a tall, dark young man with a well-trimmed black beard. "These shepherds," he said, shaking his head as he examined Fritz, "they get hip problems. It's the breeders' fault, too much inbreeding. But this old boy, I think his problem's arthritis. You say the room was cold?"

"Yes," Pearce said. "The hotel's having heating problems. Plus I had him out all day yesterday. The cold is different down here. Damper."

"I see," said Dr. Broussard, kneading Fritz's hip. "I'd like to keep him under observation for a while. If it's arthritis, we can fix him up. We've got shots these days. Have him back on his feet quick as a wink. But he has to take a series of injections. And they're expensive."

Mollie swallowed nervously. Pearce still hadn't shaved, and both of them probably looked shabby in their well-worn and wrinkled clothes. Perhaps Broussard didn't think they could afford care for Fritz.

"Money's no object," Pearce said. "I'll pay in advance." He took out his wallet and opened it. It was still stuffed with bills, their different folds indicating the different denominations.

The doctor eyed both the bills and Pearce carefully. "That won't be necessary, Mr. Goddard. I trust you. The question is can you cope without the dog? This is your wife, I take it?" He nodded toward Mollie.

Mollie took Pearce's arm protectively. "I'm not his wife. But I can watch out for him. I'll make sure nothing happens."

"It's good to know he's in such capable hands," Dr. Broussard said, smiling at her. "Why don't you call me tomorrow? It's Christmas, but I'll be in to feed and walk the animals I've got boarded. Give me a call about ten. If the shot works, you can pick him up and take him with you. But right now he should stay off his feet for a while. Rest."

"It's all right," Mollie said, looking up at Pearce's gloomy profile. She squeezed his arm. "I'll do everything that has to be done."

Broussard studied her shining face as she stared up at Pearce. "You're a very lucky man, Mr. Goddard," he said dryly.

Pearce's mouth gave an unhappy twitch at the corner. "Yeah," he said. He didn't appear to be a man who considered himself in the least lucky.

They got back into the waiting cab. The day was cold, although not as cold as yesterday. Sunshine streamed down, unimpeded by clouds, and the icicles on Dr. Broussard's roof glittered and were starting to melt, dripping bright drops.

"I want to stop at a clothing store on the way back," Pearce told the cab driver. "And I want you to wait for us."

"Store?" Mollie asked, distracted. She was still deeply upset about the dog. She couldn't stand to think of him in pain or frightened. The image of Fritz trying to stagger to his feet haunted her.

"I can't stand to spend another day in these clothes," Pearce muttered. "The next time I take off this shirt it's going to stand up and walk around the room on its cuffs. I'll buy you something, too. You've got to be feeling the same way."

"No," Mollie said, shaking her head. "I wash my things out at night." Last night, to distract herself, she had washed everything washable. Her turtleneck hadn't dried in the cold room, but her pink blouse had, though it was badly wrinkled.

Pearce sighed in exasperation. "I *want* to buy you something." He put his arm along the back of the seat.

"No," she said flatly. She was altogether too conscious of his nearness, which seemed wrong to her under the circumstances. At a time like this, she shouldn't be thinking of the impact he had on her senses. But she could feel the warmth of his lean body, and he smelled of hotel soap and shampoo.

He was such a remarkable man, she thought. She kept forgetting he was blind; it was as if he wasn't blind at all. But he was, and what was he going to do if Fritz didn't get well? That was what she had to worry about.

She stared out the window, trying to ignore Pearce's closeness and frowning in consternation. "Oh, Pearce, do you think he'll be all right? Fritz? Oh, the poor old guy."

"Mollie, the doctor sounded as if everything's going to be fine," he said reassuringly. "Try not to let it upset you."

"I didn't mean to get upset," she said miserably, not wanting to look at him. "It's just that when I got up this morning...well...I realized what day it is, and I guess I started feeling sorry for myself. Which is a really stupid thing to do, and I'm not going to do it any more, but when I saw Fritz, well...it was too much. I told myself I was going to be sensible today. I'm off to a bad start, I guess."

"You realized what day it is—what day is it?" Pearce asked, puzzlement in his voice. He was so near that his breath made her neck tingle warmly.

She was startled when his hand brushed the loose fall of her hair. "Tomorrow's Christmas," she said, surprised that he hadn't seemed to realize it. "Tonight's Christmas Eve. In our family, that's when we always celebrated. You know, gave each other our presents and hung up our stockings and all the usual things. I guess this is the first time I haven't been with them—that I've been alone. Did your family celebrate on Christmas Eve? Or Christmas Day?"

"Christmas Eve, too," he said. Gently he took a strand of her hair and wound it around his finger, toying with it. "Harry and I were too impatient to wait for Christmas Day. Especially Harry. When we were kids, he always fought to camp in the fireplace. He wanted Santa Claus to land right *on* him. Knowing Harry, he probably figured he could extort a few extra toys out of the old guy."

Mollie turned to face him. He was nearer to her than she had realized. His handsome, enigmatic face filled her field of vision, and she found herself wanting to smooth his brown hair back from his widow's peak. It was atypically mussed this morning, a short lock hanging over his forehead.

She knitted her gloved hands in her lap instead. "That's another thing I felt bad about, Pearce. What I said about your brother last night. That was terrible. I felt—I feel so guilty." She shook her head unhappily.

"Hey," he said softly, twining and untwining her hair, "it was a misunderstanding. It's over."

She wished he wouldn't play in that languid, affectionate way with her hair. It gave her a shivery feeling in the pit of her stomach and made the too-familiar shudders trace their way along her spine.

Once more she turned her face from his, not wanting to look at him because of the emotions he stirred. "Anyway," she murmured, "when you answered the door this morning, you looked so troubled, you scared me. And when I saw Fritz... I don't know. It was when he cried, I guess. That's when I lost control. I didn't mean to. I didn't mean to upset you." She was usually expert at keeping her voice even, but the memory of the dog's whimper made the quaver creep back in.

"It's all right," Pearce said, putting his arm around her and drawing her to him. "Everything's going to be fine."

Gratefully she leaned her head against his chest. The arm around her shoulders seemed strong enough to defend her from any danger in the world. She had wanted to remain aloof from him today, but she found it was impossible. It felt too fine, too right, too comforting to rest in the shelter of his arm.

"It will be fine, won't it?" she asked, wanting to be reassured. "Nothing else bad will happen, will it? Not on Christmas. And not on Christmas Eve."

Did she feel or only imagine she felt his muscles tense? She didn't know.

He was silent for a moment. All she heard was the rapid, dependable beat of his heart. He stroked her hair softly.

"No," he said at last. "Nothing else bad is going to happen to you. Not on Christmas and not on Christmas Eve. I promise."

He bent and kissed her ear, knowing that he couldn't tell her yet. Not yet.

So he held her tighter, as if by holding her, he could protect her from all unhappiness. But he knew, in his heart, what she most needed to be protected from was himself.

CHAPTER SEVEN

ALL RIGHT, PEARCE THOUGHT. He couldn't tell her now. Not on Christmas Eve and not on Christmas. He would have to wait.

How he would tell her and when he would tell her became problems that tested his considerable creativity. He had some thoughts that bordered on the outlandish—for instance, that they would part, that he would appear on her doorstep a few months later, saying a miraculous cure had been effected and he could see again. An experimental operation that he couldn't tell her about.

No, he thought, that wouldn't do. She hated lies, and all he seemed to do was become more deeply mired in them. But how could he tell her? And when? It made his every moment with her bittersweet.

He retreated into thinking about the mole. Moncrief Mole went shopping.

How does a blind man shop? Pearce wondered. He quickly discovered the answer. Such a man needed someone like Mollie Randall. Someone exactly like Mollie Randall.

One of the landmarks of the French Quarter was the old building that had once housed the Jackson Brewing Company, the home of New Orleans's famous Jax Beer. Now the building had become a mall, a multistoried complex of stores, bars, restaurants and boutiques.

Mollie was hard put to describe what she saw when they got out of the cab. "It's a big gray building, almost classic-looking," she told Pearce, holding his arm protectively. "It has white trim and big gold letters over the main entrance saying Jackson Brewing Company. And—oh, Pearce, you'd love it—it's such a dignified old building, but there are funny alligators everywhere."

New Orleans, more than any other North American city, was identified with animals. Toronto had its squirrels, New York its pigeons, San Francisco its seals, but New Orleans, as usual, beat them all in terms of the exotic.

The image of the alligator, fearsome creature of the bayous and swamps, reigned supreme in New Orleans. It was challenged only by that of the crawfish, the miniature cousin of the lobster that Cajun cooking had made into one of the continent's most succulent treats.

Over the main entrance of the Jackson brewery, perched on the portico roof, was a huge comic replica of a bright green alligator dressed as Santa Claus, waving from his sled. At a side entrance more comic alligators posed, dressed in their Christmas finery and going about their Christmas business.

Inside, commanding three stories of the interior, an elaborate display hung over the escalator system. An enormous effigy of Santa Claus was surrounded by humorous-looking alligators. There was an alligator dressed as a king, one costumed as a New Orleans chef, one as Santa's elf, one as a wizard with a pointed purple cap. Giant alligators dangled in the air over the shoppers, sporting baseball caps, or turtleneck sweaters and spectacles, or Louisiana football jerseys.

"Oh, Pearce," Mollie said excitedly, "There's even an alligator walking around greeting shoppers!"

She hugged his arm harder and tried to describe the person costumed as a huge, enormously chubby alligator dressed in a red-and-white Santa jacket, a red cap bobbing merrily on his head. The alligator grinned with funny, snaggly teeth. The expression in his large blue eyes was both benevolent and slightly deranged. He strolled among the shoppers, waving, bowing and warmly hugging the children.

In another corner of the mall, standing before a cookie shop, a quartet of people dressed in rich Renaissance garb sang Christmas madrigals.

Mollie worked hard to describe it all as vividly as she could as she steered Pearce onto the escalator, then chose a menswear shop.

"Can I trust you?" he asked satirically as he felt the fabric of the sweaters ranged before him. "You're not going to dress me in purple with green polka dots, are you?"

"It depends on how you behave," Mollie teased.

She picked out another dark green sweater for him, another white shirt, a pair of black slacks. She balked at picking out his underwear. It seemed too intimate.

"Oh, come on," he taunted. "Do something daring. Pick out some hot pink bikini briefs for me—argyle socks. A T-shirt with a naked lady printed on it."

"Underwear is underwear," Mollie said firmly. "Just tell the clerk what you want."

"Ah, you won't fiddle with my underwear at all. Unfair. I'd fiddle with yours."

"Leave my underwear out of things," she told him.

"I'd love to. I'd like you with no underwear at all. It's a sexy thought."

"Stop that," Mollie said, embarrassed but smiling.

"I can't stop it," he said innocently. "We're in New Orleans, the sexiest city in America, and I'm with the woman with the sexiest voice in the world, and she's talking to me about her underwear."

"I'm not talking about my underwear," she protested. "*You* are."

She was exasperated, but could not help thinking how handsome he looked, silhouetted against the store's Christmas display of ribbons and holly. He grinned at her with his beautiful smile, broad, white and perfect.

"What I want to talk about," he said, "is my underwear. Pick me out some briefs. Life's too short for boring underwear."

"Is that the cornerstone of your philosophy?" she asked tartly.

He lifted a derisive eyebrow. "Absolutely."

She ended up by picking out a pair of black briefs and a pair of white boxer shorts with red devils printed all over them. The devils were squat little creatures, with horns, tails and pitchforks.

"Somehow," she said wryly, looking at the shorts with the devils, "I think this style is *you.*"

Pearce insisted on buying her a fresh blouse—after all, he said, it was Christmas—and a change of lingerie. "Stop feeling it," she whispered harshly at him in the women's boutique. He was fingering a lacy bra with obvious relish. "People will think you're a weirdo."

"Fancy that," he said, his voice bland. "Me. A weirdo. Imagine that."

Oh, she thought, with a sigh that was both weary and pleasured, he was impossible, but he always made her laugh, even if it was sometimes in despair.

They headed back to the hotel. The fare on the cab's meter was so high that it horrified Mollie, but Pearce seemed unfazed.

"Look," he said. "I told you I'm going into business for myself. This is my last fling. You've been a good sport about everything else. Be a good sport about this."

"I feel guilty," Mollie muttered, clutching her packages. "You've spent too much money on me. We eat like kings and I've got the best room, and now all this cab fare...and clean clothes..."

He grinned a slow and lazy grin. "You're turning into a nag, Mollie. That's not your style. What are you trying to do? Ruin my Christmas?"

"Of course not," she protested.

"Then be happy," he said, his grin fading. "Just be happy. I'm not trying to compromise you. I swear it."

She stared at his face, startled by his sudden seriousness. She realized that she usually was happy when she was with him. Sometimes she was so happy it felt almost dangerous.

The same thing was happening today as had happened yesterday. Although her heart was supposed to be broken, she was having more fun than she'd had in a long time. It was a paradox. Perhaps, she thought, a bit frightened by the idea, her heart hadn't been broken at all. Maybe she hadn't loved Michael as much as she thought. Maybe she hadn't understood what love was.

The idea sobered her. Beside her, Pearce had gone atypically silent, his face almost brooding. She stayed silent herself, studying him. *Who are you, really?* she wanted to ask. *And why do you make me feel this way so often? As if when I'm with you, someone might open a door and show me every kind of heaven if I just stay by your side?*

Back at the hotel, they went to their separate rooms to change. Mollie was infinitely grateful for fresh lingerie and a clean, pressed blouse. They made her feel fresh and clean, perky and happy.

But she shouldn't have let him buy her clothes, she told herself, her smile dying. That was too intimate a gift. She would have to make it clear she would pay him back. She couldn't keep drifting along, accepting more and more of his generosity. Even though he'd said he didn't mean to compromise her, she couldn't feel right about all she'd taken from him.

The problem was that she was letting him treat her like a mistress, Mollie told herself sternly. That meant she could hardly be surprised if he expected her to *act* like his mistress, no matter what he said to the contrary.

No, she really must try harder to keep things under control. Pearce, unfortunately, was the kind of man designed to make things fly completely out of control with giddy abandon, to wreck all preconceptions and make all ordinary rules seem useless.

She went to his room to fetch him, resolving not to let him put her off balance again. When he opened the door, she saw that he had again cut his chin shaving. That he'd wounded himself a second time within two days dismayed her.

"Oh, Pearce," she said, shaking her head in concern, "you nicked yourself again. What's wrong? If you keep this up you'll never get back to California. You'll wither up right here from loss of blood."

Almost without her volition she reached up and gently touched his chin. The second cut was not as deep as the first, but crossed it, creating a thin, lopsided X just below his full lower lip.

She shouldn't have touched him, she thought. She'd just spent the last quarter of an hour telling herself to stay in better control of the situation. But now the feel of his skin beneath her fingers went through her like a powerful jolt of electricity. She suppressed a gasp, holding her breath.

He, too, seemed galvanized by the unexpected touch. He caught her hand and held it against his clean-shaven cheek. He bent toward her. "Mollie," he said, his voice taut, his face becoming serious, as it sometimes could.

"What?" she breathed. She felt paralyzed, as if a spell had been cast on her. She stared up into his face, almost dizzied by the power of her feeling for him.

"Nothing," he said, his voice low. He took her face between his hands. "Just... Mollie."

He bent lower and kissed her. It was a long kiss, at first gentle, then hot with yearning. She felt, dreamily, as if she could be kissed by him forever and love it, could glory in it for the rest of her life. The touch of him was like paradise.

He was the one who, at last, drew his lips away. "Mollie," he said again, with pain in his voice. He hugged her to him so tightly that there seemed something desperate in it, almost frightening. "I just want you to have a happy Christmas," he said, his tone strained. "That's all I want. So let's get out of here. Before something happens between us you'll regret."

I couldn't regret anything that happened with you, she thought, clinging to him. The thought shocked her because she knew she had finally admitted the truth, and it both dazzled and terrified her.

She was so drawn to him that the intensity of her feeling almost dizzied her. She had tried as hard as she could to deny that feeling, but his simplest touch betrayed her.

She feared, in truth, that she loved him, as mad as that might seem. And she knew, in truth, that she wanted him, as perilous as that might be. It was the first time she had ever felt such strong physical desire.

Her own passion frightened her, and when he pulled away from her, she drew back from him as well, almost shamefully. There were so many things she didn't know about this man, she thought with a chill. Too many things.

FOR A BELATED BREAKFAST, they went to the French bakery just off Jackson Square. In the window were effigies of seafood. A giant golden brown lobster baked of bread dough crouched among the cookies and pastries. Beside it sat an enormous baked crab, looking so flaky and succulent that it made visions of butter dance in Mollie's head. The crab had a sprig of holly pinched in its toasty claw.

I love this city, she thought with a surge of feeling, smiling down at the two whimsical bread sculptures. *Because this city loves laughter.*

She and Pearce sat at a small table with wrought iron legs, drinking New Orleans's café au lait and eating French pastries. Outside, a lone musician braved the cold, playing Christmas carols on a large brass tuba. *Oompah, ompooh,* came its muted notes, drifting through the fragrant air of the bakery.

"This is the strangest Christmas I've ever had," Mollie said, shaking her head. In the corner of the bakery, stretched out on a table covered with a red cloth was a real alligator, stuffed and over four feet long. On its head was a crown of poinsettias. Its mouth was open and filled with holly. A chain of sleigh bells was coiled around its tail.

"It's strange," Pearce agreed, sipping his coffee. "But it's not bad. Is it? You're not still lonesome for your family, are you?"

She shrugged, looking out the window at the bundled-up tuba player. "I miss them, of course—but I'm not lonesome. It's like being in a magic land here. I'm glad you convinced me to come. To not turn back."

He held his coffee mug in both hands. His black glasses seemed to be staring at her. Once more she marveled at how strong and sensitive his tanned hands were, how mobile and changeable his mouth was. "You're not the kind to turn back," he said. "You weren't made for retreat. You were created to go forward, to see new things, take chances."

She smiled a bit shyly. She pushed her red-gold hair back off her shoulder. "Well, my father would be happy to hear you say that. His actions might not always prove it, but he always says life is for taking chances."

Pearce nodded. "He's right."

She thought of Michael and her smile faded. It was one of the few times she'd thought of Michael all morning. "Some people," she said slowly, "think wanting to be an actress is—is stupid. That it means taking too *many* chances. That people like me aren't very smart. What we want is impossible. We're asking for disappointment."

He reached across the table and took her hand. Delight, simple and complete, raced through her body at his touch.

"There have to be dreamers, Mollie. Nothing beautiful—maybe even nothing funny—would exist without dreamers."

He squeezed her hand, then released it quickly, as if he had no right to touch her. She stared at him in perplexity.

Once again she was intrigued by the quicksilver changes of which his strong face was capable. At one moment he looked like the sort of man who would take lonely walks in the moonlight and write sonnets. In the next moment he could look like someone athletic and sensual, the sort of man who lived entirely in his body, not his thoughts. And now, for reasons Mollie couldn't understand, he looked pensive, uneasy, filled with too many shifting emotions, none of them happy.

"Does it bother you," she hazarded, "being alone at Christmas? I mean, not having a family?"

His mercurial grin crossed his lips. "I'm used to it."

She squared her shoulders, pushed her hair back again. "And your fiancée?" she said carefully. "Didn't you feel . . . close to her? I mean, you *were* engaged."

He shrugged and made a sighing sound of disgust. "No. I thought she'd do. That's all I ever expected from a woman—that she'd be all right. But she didn't do. I'm a loner. That's what I found out about myself from that rotten experience. I'm not the sort of man who...should get involved. My life is too chancy now. That's how I want it and how it's got to be."

"Oh," Mollie said. "I see. I mean, I understand."

She thought perhaps she did understand. Was this the "talk" he'd kept saying he wanted to have with her? Was it the standard speech of such men? "I'm a rogue male— I go on my way, do my own thing, take no passengers with me. I make no promises. I belong to nobody. I won't belong to you."

She stared into her empty coffee cup. "My own life is pretty chancy," she said. "And that's the way I want it, too. My—my boyfriend couldn't quite come to grips with it. I guess your fiancée couldn't, either."

"Right."

They were silent for a long time. Outside, the tuba player went *oompah, oompah, oompah.* Inside, the alligator posed on the corner table, his Santa hat at a jaunty angle, his tail bright with sleigh bells.

"You've never told me what you really do," Mollie said at last. "What your work is." She looked up and saw that he wasn't smiling.

"I can't tell you what I do," he said. "I'd have to lie about it."

In surprise, she drew in her breath slightly. Her hands tightened about the empty mug. She tried to laugh but didn't quite succeed. "You sound like a spy—or a criminal," she said, trying to joke.

She found, however, that she couldn't smile, and neither did he. "I'm not a spy," he said. "I'm not a criminal. It's just that right now I can't tell you, and I'd rather not talk about it."

She frowned in confusion, again not knowing what to say. "Well," she finally said, "I guess I'd rather not know than have you lie. I'd hate it if you lied to me. I guess that's the one thing I couldn't stand. I couldn't go through that again."

He leaned toward her, his expression atypically earnest. "Look," he said. "Let's just have a good Christmas, all right? A great time, that's all. Let's make that our number-one priority."

Mollie looked out the big window of the bakery. The fronds of the palm trees in Jackson Square were shivering in the winter wind, and the sky was a cold, brilliant blue. Across the room the alligator stretched on its scarlet cloth grinned its mocking grin, its teeth full of holly.

She was in New Orleans for all too short a time with a man about whom she knew little and with whom she was foolishly falling in love.

On Christmas afternoon, tomorrow, she would fly back to New York. He would fly to Los Angeles. She might never see him again. It was that simple and that final. But until tomorrow afternoon, they were together.

Together, she thought. They had one more day. And one more night.

"How do they say it?" she asked, lifting her chin. *"Laissez les bons temps rouler?* Let the good times roll."

THEY WALKED, THEY TOOK a carriage ride, they rode on the famous streetcar called Desire, although now it was actually a bus. Mollie told Pearce how much she loved the play by Tennessee Williams titled after that streetcar.

They had stopped in a bar so that Mollie could taste New Orleans's most famous drink, the potent "hurricane," but Mollie didn't like the touristy atmosphere of the place, and Pearce grumbled that it was too noisy for him. Hundreds of beer steins hung from the ceiling, as if inviting the whole world to come in and drink, and the piano player pounded relentlessly, determined to overwhelm the room with jangling show tunes.

They escaped and instead walked quietly beside the broad, surprisingly blue Mississippi River. The sea gulls swooped above them, and on the water a fancy riverboat, lacy with Victorian gingerbread, bobbed next to soberer, more mundane vessels.

Pearce surprised her by having her walk him to a hotel back in the Quarter called La Maison de Ville. They strolled through the small but elegant lobby, decorated with a tree trimmed all in gold and silver, and into the hotel's courtyard.

Small deserted tables and chairs of wrought iron stood on the courtyard's gray stone floor, and garlands and wreathes of pine, tied with red ribbons, hung on its brick walls and from its delicate grillwork balconies.

A frozen fountain stood in its center, surrounded by rosebushes that were covered with clear plastic to protect them from the cold. Their leaves were bright and healthy green. A banana tree hadn't fared as well. Its leaves were dark and withered, and two large branches had snapped off.

A banana tree, a fountain of ice and live roses, thought Mollie, how odd and how wonderful.

"Look over there," Pearce said, putting his arm around her. "There should be a door marked 'nine.' It's the door to a famous room."

Mollie looked up at him inquiringly, not knowing why he had brought her here. Then she stared at the double door, painted black and marked with a metal 9. It had a brick threshold and twelve small, gleaming windows. A cluster of pine boughs, ribboned with red, hung next to it.

"In that room," he said solemnly, "your man lived. That playwright you love so much. Tennessee Williams. Right there. That's the place where he wrote *A Streetcar Named Desire*. And this is the view he looked out on every day while he did it. This fountain, these bricks, these balconies."

Mollie hung onto his arm, too moved to speak. She knew little about Williams's life except that he had lived in New Orleans for a time, but she knew every one of his plays and was awed by them.

Of all of them, *A Streetcar Named Desire* was her favorite. She had seen the movie with Marlon Brando and Vivien Leigh a dozen times. Someday, when she was older, she prayed she would be good enough to play the part Vivien Leigh had played, the wonderful, demanding, heartbreaking, immortal role of Blanche Dubois.

"The way you talked, you sounded like *A Streetcar Named Desire* sort of girl," he said gruffly. "I thought you might want to see this."

"Oh, Pearce," she managed to say. "I didn't know. I guess I never thought about it. I knew he'd lived in the Quarter, but I never thought the place might still be standing. This is like going to a shrine for me! To think he walked on these very stones. That he looked out those windows and saw this fountain, the bricks in these walls...."

"But he never saw it this cold," he said wryly, smiling down at her.

She was so delighted that she couldn't stop herself from hugging his arm. "He wrote so many great parts," she said in awe. "Oh, to see where he lived, to be here— this is the best Christmas present anyone's ever given me. Oh, thank you, Pearce, it's wonderful."

Impulsively she reached up and kissed him on his chin, precisely where his two shaving cuts crossed.

"We'll have a drink in the lobby to celebrate and to let you soak up some more atmosphere." He seemed pleased by her pleasure. He gave her his lopsided grin. "And I have the feeling you could quote me yards of dialogue from the play."

"I can," she laughed. "Be careful or I will."

"Do it, Mollie," he challenged, putting his arm around her and hugging her closer to him. "Stand here on his doorstep and recite his lines. It'll be like wishing his ghost a merry Christmas."

"Let's see," she said, shaking her head as she thought. Her bright hair fluttered in the wind. "Oh, there's that wonderful exchange between Blanche and Mitch. He's fallen in love with her, but she's not what he thinks. She's created so many illusions—she's had to, in order to survive. He says, 'You lied to me, Blanche.' And she begs him, 'Don't say I lied to you.' And he says, 'Lies! Lies, inside and out! All lies.' And she says, 'Never inside! I never lied in my heart.'''

The grin died from Pearce's face. The arm he wrapped around her grew rigid, as if with tension.

"Is something wrong?" she asked in concern, puzzled by the change in him.

"Let's get a drink and get warm," he said. He dropped his arm away from her shoulders. She shivered without knowing why.

THE AFTERNOON HAD GROWN warmer and the streets and sidewalks began to fill with artists and musicians. A white-faced mime pretended to walk against the wind. Four men and a curly-haired woman played and sang folk music in the middle of Bourbon Street.

A man who called himself a "healing artist" was giving a neck massage to an elderly giggling tourist. On the corner of Bienville Street, by the lazy iron facade of the Old Absinth House, a group of black musicians were playing jazz.

The breeze from the river was warmer now, although the thin sunlight was beginning to fail and the thousands of lights of the French Quarter were coming on. Mollie paused almost involuntarily before another shop window filled with masks.

"What's caught your fancy now?" Pearce teased.

"These masks," Mollie said, musing. "I never saw so many. Someday maybe I'll come back for Mardi Gras."

The masks filled the window with a gaudy rainbow of colors. There was one of bright blue feathers decorated with silver tinsel, one of iridescent peacock feathers, one of scarlet sequins and another of gold, crowned with black-and-gold pheasant feathers.

"It's a city of masks," she said thoughtfully. In the shop's other window, on the other side of the door, stood a mannequin dressed in an elaborate costume, red velvet and pink spangles and ropes of gold. She wore wings of shining gold and a velvet hat with a large golden crescent moon mounted on it. Her eyes were masked with glittering gold. "A city of disguises. Sometimes there seems something almost sinister about that."

"It's just the way things are here," he said, his voice almost harsh. "Come on. It's also a city of restaurants. Pick a good one. It's Christmas Eve. We might as well make the most of it."

"It seems strange without Fritz," Mollie said, taking Pearce's arm again. "I miss him."

"Yeah," he said, patting her gloved hand. "Me, too."

She glanced up at him. "Pearce, what will you do if— if he doesn't get well? I mean well enough to make sure you get home safely? The vet said he should rest."

Pearce shrugged impatiently. "I can manage."

"What time are you supposed to leave tomorrow?" she asked. "I mean, we both leave tomorrow. But if I had to, I—I could try to change my ticket...to leave after you do. Just to make sure you're on the plane all right and everything. You know. So you won't have to rely on strangers."

He gave a rough sigh. "Don't worry about me, all right? Don't . . . fuss. I'll be fine. It's not like I can't take care of myself, all right?"

"I'm sorry," she said earnestly. "I didn't mean to sound like a nag. I just wanted to make sure—"

He stopped, cutting her off. He turned and bent over her, taking her face between his hands. Once more he had an unaccountable tenseness in his face. "I know what you want to do. You want to make sure I'm all right. I guarantee it: I'll be all right. All I want is for us to have fun tonight. We don't have much time left. Let's make it count for something. I want your memories of this to be good. I want them to be happy. I don't want to hear you worry. I want to hear you laugh."

His gloved hands were cool against her face, but his breath was warm. The muscles in his jaw were rigid.

"Pearce," she said, not understanding the expression on his face. "You're so serious—"

"I'm serious about having fun," he said. "That's all I've ever been serious about in my life. So pick a restaurant, all right?"

She nodded, swallowing hard. She finally chose a restaurant that specialized in oysters and seafood. Its name was Desire.

"LISTEN," HE SAID over dessert, which was bread pudding with whiskey sauce, "I know you're a serious actress. That you love Tennessee Williams and all that. But an actress has to eat. I said I have connections in the animation field. After this is over—Christmas and everything—I might get in touch."

A feeling of happiness spread through Mollie's chest, unfolding like a beautiful fan. They might stay in touch. Perhaps tomorrow wouldn't be the end of everything. Things might not be over between them, not completely.

"This project I have in mind needs a girl with a voice like yours," he said, his mouth turning down at one corner. "It's a strange part. But it's big. She's a mink. That wouldn't put you off, would it? Playing a mink?"

"A mink?" Mollie laughed. "Are you kidding? I'm going back to New York to play a *germ,* remember. A mink is leaps and bounds up the evolutionary scale. I'd love to play a mink."

He almost smiled. "Write down your name and address and phone number for me. And your agent's."

She opened her purse, took out a pen and scribbled the information he wanted on the inside of a matchbook that sat in the table's crystal ashtray. She opened his hand and placed the matchbook in it.

He put it in the inside pocket of his jacket. Mollie swallowed nervously. What if he misplaced it? What if he then tried to find her and couldn't? New York was a massive city, full of hundreds of women named Randall.

"Does this mean we might...work together somehow, you and I?" she asked, forcing her voice to stay even and calm.

"We might," he said. "If you want to. But that's something we'll talk about another time. Not tonight. Not at Christmas."

"You're a writer—aren't you?" Mollie said with a sudden flash of inspiration. "This is some kind of story you're working on. That's why you knew all about Tennessee Williams. Why you have the kind of imagination you do. Because you're a writer."

"Kind of," Pearce said vaguely. It was true enough, he thought. He was a writer, among other things. Foremost he was an artist, but to animate, he had to have a story, characters, a plot, and they had obsessed him for years.

He had tried his best to be honorable today. He had wanted to tell her the truth, then realized he couldn't; the timing was wrong. He had kept his eyes closed, but now he yielded to temptation and opened them.

Oh, God, he thought, her hair was like a cloud of fire around her face. Her beautiful, special, freckled face. Light and sight seemed so foreign to him after his long day of self-imposed darkness that looking at her actually hurt him. To see her face was like having a knife go through him.

What was he going to tell this woman? And how? And when? What sort of impossible mess had he gotten himself into and how was he going to get out of it unscathed and without hurting her?

He sighed in exasperation and threw his napkin down on the table. Reluctantly he shut his eyes again. "Let's go," he said shortly.

He stood, fumbling to button his jacket. She helped him, but she did it without fuss. Good Lord, he thought, he wanted nothing more than to take her back to the hotel and make love to her all night long.

But he couldn't. She would never forgive him if he did that and later she found out he had lied about his eyes. *Merry Christmas, Mollie,* he thought. *My present is that I won't make love to you. It's only going to kill me.*

Out on the street she took his arm and stared up at the Christmas lights hanging over the street. She was quiet because he was quiet. He seemed bothered by something, and she couldn't understand what or why.

She wondered if he would try to make love to her again tonight, and knew that if he did, this time she would not refuse. She could not say no to him if he asked. It was foolish and dangerous, she knew, but she had to admit she had fallen in love with him. It was a feeling such as she had never before experienced. She had never felt this way about Michael. She had never felt this way about anyone.

She found herself pausing once more at the shop window filled with masks. Pearce stopped, too. "What are you looking at?" he asked.

"The masks again," she said, looking at the sparkling red sequined one. It was trimmed with black feathers that stood up like long, curving horns.

"Why do they fascinate you so much?" he asked, his voice low. He squeezed her arm slightly, and even that small motion sent tremors dancing through her.

"I don't know," she murmured, shaking her head.

"Do I need to buy you one?" he asked. "For your Christmas present?"

She looked at their reflections in the shop window. Their images seemed to float over the masks like ghosts. "Oh, no," she said, "you've done too much already. I couldn't let you do—"

A hoarse cry cut her off. "Stop! Thief! Stop that man! Him!"

Mollie turned around in confusion. She heard the sound of rapid footsteps growing nearer, almost thundering.

"Stop him! He grabbed my wife's purse!"

Mollie turned the other way, disoriented. Suddenly she saw the cause of the commotion: two men pounding down the sidewalk toward her and Pearce. A ragged-looking, lean man with a woman's purse clutched to his chest was pushing his way through the sidewalk crowds. A large man, middle-aged but obviously athletic, was hot on his trail.

The thief knocked into a woman so hard she fell to the sidewalk. He lost his balance from the impact and lurched forward, knocking into Mollie. Pearce had grabbed her to protect her and moved her swiftly and safely against the store's brick wall. Then he lunged at the man, bringing him down in a tackle.

The thief tried to rise, and he swung his fist at Pearce, smashing off his dark glasses. Pearce drew back his own fist and struck the man a powerful blow on the jaw. The thief sank back onto the sidewalk, dazed but not unconscious. The big man who had been in pursuit leaned down and hauled the robber to his feet. He snatched the purse from the man's enfeebled grasp.

The big man's graying hair was disheveled and he was breathing hard. He looked frightened and out of breath, as if too much excitement and effort had suddenly drained his strength. "I need a policeman," he panted.

"There's one coming," Pearce said. He saw a stocky black policeman in a dark blue uniform rounding the corner. He also realized that the thief was coming out of his grogginess and was probably thinking of bolting again. "You flag him down. I'll hold your friend." Pearce stepped behind the robber, twisting his arm in a hammerlock. "Try to run again," he whispered in the man's ear, "and I'll break your arm off." He gave the arm a jerk for emphasis and the man grimaced.

"Are you all right?" he asked Mollie, glancing at her. The man had crashed into her with enough force that he must have knocked the breath out of her.

She stared back at him, breathing shallowly. Her face was perfectly white, as white as he had ever seen a human face. Her freckles stood out like little stars against her pallor. Her silly little hat had been knocked askew and her red-gold hair tumbled over her shoulders in beautiful disarray. Her eyes were very wide; they seemed preternaturally blue in the whiteness of her face, and she was gazing at him in sheer horror.

Suddenly he understood. The dark glasses lay in the gutter, one of the lenses cracked. He looked at Mollie and she looked back at him, and she knew.

The cries had made him open his eyes without thinking. He had seen the thief before she did and had grabbed her to protect her. He had tackled the man unerringly, and when his glasses were knocked off, he had hit him just as unerringly.

He had seen the tourist giving chase to the thief and told him that a policeman was coming, and then he'd taken charge of the thief so the older man didn't have to exert himself anymore.

Mollie's full mouth trembled. Her jaw quavered dangerously. She stared into his eyes, which were a clear, deep green beneath his arched brows. They were deep-set eyes, with rather hooded lids and long dark lashes.

He looked at Mollie, and she looked at him.

"You can see," she said, her husky voice almost toneless. "You've been lying to me all along. You can see, can't you?"

He swallowed, staring over the man's shoulder at her. He kept his eyes locked with hers. Never before had he seen such an expression on a woman's face. It spoke a thousand things to him. Mostly it communicated a sense of betrayal so deep that it wrenched his stomach as if someone had hit him hard enough to break something within him.

He nodded. "Yes," he said.

He swallowed again, hating the look on her face and hating herself for putting it there. He, usually quick with words, could only think of the tritest ones: "Let me explain."

But he couldn't explain. She had turned and was running down the street, running as swiftly as she could, her long hair streaming behind her, reflecting the Christmas lights in sparks of fire.

He couldn't chase her because he was still holding the thief, who was starting to struggle again, and the policeman had arrived and was bombarding him with questions.

Pearce couldn't hear the questions. He just kept staring after Mollie, even after she had disappeared from view.

CHAPTER EIGHT

BLINDLY, ALMOST WILDLY, Mollie made her way back to the hotel. She gathered her few belongings, rolled them into a bundle, thrust them under her arm and locked the door behind her.

She paused to count her money. She still had the fifty dollars from cashing the check at the Dallas airport. Somehow, someway, she would make the money see her through her final night and morning in New Orleans. She would find the cheapest hotel possible. She would take a bus, not a cab, to the airport. She would go hungry if she had to.

She was running down the curving stairs, desperate to leave the scene of her folly. It was on the stairs that she encountered Pearce. He was breathing hard, as if he'd been running. He seized her by the arms.

She hated seeing him, but once more she was amazed by the live, quick greenness of his eyes. She looked up into them and thought, irrationally, that his eyes matched his face far too well.

They were beautiful eyes, the clear, dark green of jewels, but she could tell they were as changeable as everything else about him. Now they burned with an intensity she didn't trust, because she could trust nothing about him.

"I can explain," he said, pulling her closer to him, not letting her escape. "It was an experiment—a joke almost. It got out of hand."

"Some experiment," Mollie stormed, trying to push away from him. "Some joke. You lied. You lied and lied. You were nothing but lies—inside and out."

"Stop it," he hissed, gripping her arms more tightly and pulling her back to him. "I tried to tell you, but things kept happening. Last night Irina had you too upset. This morning it was Fritz. You said you didn't want anything else bad to happen—it was Christmas. I decided to wait to tell you."

"Irina." She practically spat the word. Her hair was tumbled, falling into her eyes, and she tried, unsuccessfully, to shake it out of her way. "Irina's lucky to be rid of you."

Tears welled into her eyes, but they were tears of rage, not sorrow, and she shook her head again, fiercely willing the tears to vanish. "And *Fritz,*" she said from between her teeth. "I almost cried for you because of poor Fritz. Where did you get him? Did you steal him from a real blind man? Along with his tin cup and his pencils? I *hate* you. I really do hate you."

"Mollie," Pearce said in a harsh, low voice. His eyes flashed like dark green fires. "The dog is mine. He was my uncle's. My uncle was blind. He died. I had to get Fritz home. And I wanted to know what it was like to be blind. I'm an animator. I want to make a feature. About a mole. A blind mole in New Orleans—a detective. And a mink. That's . . . one of the reasons I liked having you close at first. Your voice. I did this—the blind thing—to understand the mole, but you made me understand the mink, too."

She looked at him with undisguised disgust. Her lip curled. "Mole?" she challenged, a sneer in her voice. "A mink? *Cartoon* characters? That's all this has been to you? Playing with cartoon characters?"

"No," he said fiercely. He looked as if he wanted to shake her and only the greatest self-control kept him from doing so. "At first, maybe. But then I didn't want to hurt you—I was trying to find a way to tell you—"

"You'd never have told me anything," Mollie raged, shaking her head impotently. "You were enjoying yourself too much. Lying, lying, lying. And you were *good* at it."

Her lip curled more bitterly and she felt the hated tears burning as she stared up into his eyes, his beautiful, keen, green eyes. "I helped you drink your coffee," she said with revulsion. "I helped you hold the cup. In restaurants I cut up your food for you. I led you around as if *I* were your dog. I picked out your clothes for you. You even made me pick out your *underwear*. What laughs you must have been having. What fun. Poor, stupid Mollie. And in your spare time you did nothing except try to get me into bed. Out of boredom, I suppose. No other woman was around."

This time he did shake her. "Stop it," he ordered, his mouth twisting in anger. "It wasn't fun. I wasn't laughing. Yes, I wanted you in my bed. What sane man wouldn't? But I wasn't going to try to get you there anymore. I wouldn't trick you into doing it. I respected you too much. Listen to me. Listen to me, dammit."

His voice, his face, the way he touched her was so passionate that Mollie could bear it no more. "You don't respect anything," she cried, wrenching away from him. "You did this whole thing for a—a lousy, wretched *mole*. A nasty thing that lives under the ground. Well, you should tunnel under there yourself and live with the other worms."

He let her tear herself away because the only way he could have kept her in his grasp would have hurt her. Her face was still white, but she was a formidable woman in anger, so teeming with emotion she seemed explosive. He felt explosive himself.

"He's not a 'lousy, wretched mole,'" Pearce retorted defensively. "He's going to be the greatest mole in the history of the universe. And I'm the one who has to make him live. Didn't you ever study for a part?"

"Oh, a *part*," Mollie said with loathing. She gave a cynical laugh. "I don't even know if you're lying now. You're probably not even an animator. You might be anything—you might be a—a Martian. I don't know and I don't care. The one thing I know is that you're a liar."

She turned on her heel, wheeling away from him.

"I *am* an animator," he yelled after her. "I worked for ten years at the Disney studio. And four at TAS! Now I'm finally on my own, doing what I have to do."

"I don't care where you worked," Mollie cried. She stopped at the foot of the stairs long enough to draw off her garnet ring. "And I don't want to be in your debt for anything." She held the ring towards him, but he refused to take it. "Take this. It was my mother's, but sell it. Use it to pay for the food I ate and the bed I slept in. I'd rather lose it than owe you a penny. *Take* it."

Still he refused to open his hand and take it. Furiously, she flung the ring at him with all her might. It went wild, bouncing off the silken, striped wallpaper and landing in the thick carpeting at his feet.

She started to stalk away through the lobby.

"Mollie," he cried, his voice taut with anger.

She ignored him and she ignored the frank stares of the couple who stood in the lobby and had been watching the whole heated exchange.

"Snake," she muttered from between clenched teeth as she straight-armed the heavy front door into opening. "Lying, two-faced snake."

A cab was going by, slowly passing the hotel's front entrance. She hailed it and climbed in without waiting for the driver to get out and open the door for her. She slammed the door with vehemence, as if slamming it against every memory of Pearce.

"Where to?" the driver said.

"The cheapest hotel you know of around here," she said coldly, hugging her small bundle of clothes. She should have thrown the clothes at Pearce, too, she thought hotly. It irked her to be wearing a blouse he had bought, lingerie he had paid for. It made her flesh burn and itch.

"Lady," the driver said, shaking his head, "I don't think you'd *want* to stay at the cheapest hotel I know. There's some kind of scary places around here."

"I'm not scared," she said, steel in her voice. And what, indeed, did she have to be frightened of? The worst had already happened to her.

The hotel didn't seem to have a name. Outside its weather-beaten door, an ancient neon sign sputtered out the letters *otel*. The *H* was dark and dead, the flickering *o* rapidly expiring.

Her room was surprisingly cheap. It was also small, damp, cold, dirty, and had no hot water. The water pipes had frozen and burst. All night long the man in the next room coughed.

It was the sort of hotel, Mollie realized grimly, that she had thought existed only in depressing movies, the sort of room in which the rumpled hero knows he has sunk as low as he can go, and his next move will be one of desperation.

Her next move, she thought, lying on the narrow bed, hugging herself against the cold, would simply be to go back to New York. She would be a germ and she would wait tables and she would do whatever she had to do to survive.

But she would call Clytie Prokopoulos and tell her never, ever, under any circumstances, would she accept an offer of work from a man named Pearce Goddard. He had probably been lying about that, too, she thought unhappily. Getting her a job in animation had probably been merely another lie to grease her descent into his bed.

The man next door coughed hoarsely and Mollie rolled over, burying her face in the lumpy pillow. And she would have gone to Pearce's bed tonight if he had asked, fool that she was. She would have gone willingly and happily, borne on tides of emotion she would have regretted for the rest of her life.

Hot tears squeezed from between her tightly shut lids. She was a fool, and she was the stupidest kind of fool, for she had made exactly the same mistake twice. She had fallen in love with a man who didn't exist, a man who was an illusion.

First there had been Michael, she thought, clenching her fist. That experience had been horrid enough. But Michael's lies had been small, cowardly and somehow pathetic. She had thought she loved him. But the Michael she thought she loved did not, in truth, exist.

Pearce was different; Pearce was worse, she thought, brushing away the angry tears. Pearce's lies had been large, bold and outrageous. Somehow, against all her wishes and common sense, he had made her fall in love with him. He was funny and irreverent and smart and charming, and he could be gentle or he could be forceful, and he had made Michael seem like a boy Mollie had known only in a dream—one that was fading fast away.

But Pearce, too, was not what he seemed. He had been lying when they met; he would have probably been lying when they parted. If it hadn't been for the accident in the street, she might never have known he could see. The first time she had looked into those clear green eyes she had instinctively known they missed little, that they saw things far more clearly than most eyes did.

But he had lied.

She beat her fist fiercely against the pillow. What was wrong with her? Was it some sort of perverse talent that she had? Did she have an unerring instinct for being attracted to men incapable of telling the truth?

She put her fist against her hot face and bit her thumb, as if that pain could make her forget the pain in her heart. She had spent slightly less than three days with Pearce. They had been the most confounding, yet the happiest days of her life. But all of that joy had been built on falsehoods.

She bit the knuckle of her thumb harder. And the absurd part, the horrible part, was that he had done it for the sake of a *mole*. A stupid mole that wasn't even real, only a cartoon, a figment of his imagination.

She refused to cry anymore, she told herself furiously. She refused to cry because a man had lied to her over a mole. It was ridiculous.

She tried to remember all her father's handy maxims on courage, and grace under pressure, and keeping one's chin up.

It didn't help. In spite of her best efforts, she kept on crying as she had never cried for Michael, had never cried for anyone.

The man next door coughed, and someone nearby was playing a blues song on a tinny radio. A woman's strong voice, flecked by static, sang, "What Kind of Man is This?"

SHE LEFT THE HOTEL as soon as she could the next morning, shortly after dawn. She hadn't slept well and she didn't feel safe, in spite of the lock on her door. All night long the man had coughed and someone else, perhaps too lonely to sleep, had played the blues and paced the hall as if in despair.

She tidied herself as best she could, brushed out her hair until it crackled, put on her coat and left, grateful to leave the cramped and musty room behind her. It had been the worst Christmas Eve of her life.

Her plane didn't take off until two in the afternoon, so she wandered aimlessly down Bourbon Street. It was not crowded this early in the morning; it had an air of quiet and many of the shops were closed.

It would be quiet all day, instinct told her. Even there, in the French Quarter, where the party never ended, it would be quieter than usual. Because it was Christmas. People were home with their families, their loved ones.

Loved ones, she thought unhappily. She stopped in front of the store with the window full of masks, the place where she had learned the truth about Pearce.

She looked at all the masks again. The one with the peacock feathers, the one with the pheasant feathers, the one with silver tinsel, the one with scarlet sequins. The scarlet one, with its horns of black feathers, reminded her irrationally of devils and of Pearce. She could see her reflection in the window, floating dimly over the masks.

She shook her head. Masks. Disguises. Deceptions. Lies.

A man's voice came from behind her. It was low and gruff. "You lost your hat. Aren't you cold?"

She stiffened. She kept staring in the window at the masks. Another image swam in the glass, of a man standing behind her. It was Pearce. Her heart felt as if it had turned into a cold, dead stone that threatened to crush her chest. She raised her chin in defiance and tried to keep her face blank.

"I said you lost your hat," he repeated. "On the stairs last night. Aren't you cold? Or didn't you even miss it?"

She raised her chin higher still and kept her back to him. "I didn't notice it was gone," she said, her voice clipped. "Go away. Leave me alone."

"No," he said with surprising vehemence. "I won't go away. And I won't leave you alone. I've been looking for you all night long. Where in hell did you go?"

"None of your business." She tossed her head so that her hair fluttered in the cool wind. She supposed she actually *was* cold. She hadn't noticed.

He took her by the shoulders and turned her around to face him. Impatiently she shook herself free from his hands. "Don't touch me," she said, almost growling the words.

"Put on your hat," he ordered. He drew her knit cap from his jacket pocket and thrust it at her.

She glared at him, took it and put it on. He hadn't shaved and the wind had tousled his usually immaculate hair.

She still was not used to seeing his eyes, those almost mystically green eyes, and now their expression was so intent it rent her heart. She looked away. As little as she had seen his eyes, she knew they would haunt her for the rest of her life. She ducked her head and began to walk away from him, her step determined.

"I've got your mother's ring, too," he said. "You might as well take that back, as well."

"Keep it," Mollie said, without pausing or looking back at him. "I told you. I don't want to owe you *anything*."

"Mollie," he called after her, "don't be so damned stubborn. It's your mother's ring. I can't take it."

She would not answer him, she could not answer him. There was a small restaurant open on the corner and she ducked into it. Relentlessly, he followed her.

It was dark inside, the walls of aged brick. Mollie stalked aimlessly toward the back of the restaurant, where the shadows were thickest. Pearce caught up to her and took her by the elbow.

He turned her and bent so that her eyes were forced to meet his. His green eyes blazed. The shaving cuts on his chin, she noticed dazedly, were starting to heal already. She remembered feeling sorry for him because he had cut himself.

"What are you staring at?" he demanded. "Why are you giving me that look?"

"I'm wondering what kind of an idiot would shave himself with his eyes shut," she said savagely. "I suppose that's how you cut yourself, isn't it? Pretending to be a *mole*."

"Listen to me, Mollie," he said, the muscles in his jaw working with emotion. "There's no law that says a man can't pretend to be a mole."

"You're impossible," she said. "Get away from me."

"I want you to understand. You were in trouble. You needed help. You'd never have taken it from me if you thought I could see. I didn't mean any harm."

She jerked her chin upward rebelliously. "That's what people always say after they've done the harm, isn't it? That they didn't mean to do it."

"I tried to tell you. I was going to tell you. But you made me think I should wait until after Christmas—"

"I don't want your explanations," she said with passion. Her voice quavered with emotion and she let it, glad to show him how angry she was. "I don't want your excuses. I don't want anything to do with you. You have a woman who wants you in California. You have another one in Tampa. I don't understand what you want with me. You've had your fun. Leave me alone."

She pulled her elbow away from his grasp. "Leave me alone," she ordered, breathing hard, "or I'll call for help. I'll have you thrown out of here. I—I'll call the police on you."

"You're right," he said, fire flashing deep in his eyes. "I *don't* know what I want with you. I haven't got the time for this kind of thing. The next three years of my life are spoken for. I have work to do. I don't have time to keep trying to explain something to a woman who won't listen to reason. There are certain subjects on which your head is hard as a rock, and I'd probably have better luck going out and talking to a real rock."

"Oh, fine," Mollie said, her voice strained with anger. "You lie and lie, and then you accuse me of having a head like a rock."

"Look," he said, "I was trying to be a decent sort and apologize. And tell you...well, one of the reasons I kept wanting you around was your voice. I want you to think about it. When you . . . cool down. I'll be in touch with your agent. So maybe all this wasn't wasted, all right? I've got the character I want, and you can get a job out of it. Nobody's hurt and we both profit.''

Mollie drew herself up to her full height. She pulled her coat more tightly around herself. His words made her angrier than anything he'd said before. It was as if nothing emotional had happened between them. The only thing he valued, the only thing that he didn't want to lose was her voice.

"I'd *starve* before I'd work with you," she said. "I'd go home to Minnesota and wait tables for the rest of my life. I'd give up acting forever."

She turned again and strode almost ruthlessly back toward the restaurant's front door. "No," he shouted after her, contempt in his voice. "You wouldn't. You couldn't quit what you do any more than I can. You're the one who's lying now."

She ignored him and pushed the door open, stepping back onto the street.

This time Pearce didn't follow her. He went and stood against the restaurant's small mahogany bar. He glanced at the antique clock over the bar. It was hardly nine o'clock. He didn't care. "Give me a whiskey," he said in disgust to the bartender. "Straight up."

"Woman trouble?" the bartender asked mildly. He was a handsome black man who wore a red sleeve garter decorated with a sprig of holly. He had watched the furious exchange between Pearce and Mollie with a professionally blank face.

"Right," Pearce said grimly, staring out the door.

"Too bad on Christmas," the bartender said philosophically. "But take my advice. Don't worry about it. Women are pretty much alike. Lose one, find another. They're not that different."

"Right," Pearce said again, still glaring at the door. He drank the whiskey down in two swallows.

She's saved me a lot of trouble, walking out like that, he told himself. What did he need with her at this point in his life? He'd miss her voice, but there were other voices in the world.

He fingered the garnet ring in his pocket. He'd send it back to Clytie Prokopoulas or whatever her name was, to give to Mollie. He'd never have to see the girl again. He was better off without her. He was free.

MOLLIE SAT FOR A LONG time in front of the Café du Monde, nursing a mug of café au lait and watching the jugglers. They were the same pair she had seen on the street the other day. They tossed flaming torches back and forth as easily as other young men might toss baseballs.

Farther down the street the black man in the Santa Claus suit was playing "It's a Blue Christmas Without You" on his saxophone. A girl with long blond hair had set up an easel and was trying to sell caricatures to the tourists.

Today all the street performers struck Mollie as absurd and a little pathetic, playing in the bitter cold to such a small audience. But, she wondered, were they any more absurd than she was?

I'm alone in New Orleans on Christmas and I'm broke, Mollie thought glumly. *Everything I've done lately either fails or is wrong. What kind of mess have I made of my life?*

If she went back to New York, all she had to look forward to was her part as a germ. She'd made a fool of herself over a lying man who didn't care for her, and worse, it was the second time this month she had done it.

Maybe what she'd told Pearce was right, she thought, shaking her head. Perhaps Michael hadn't been cowardly at all, only practical. She should give up her stupid dreams. She should go back to Minnesota and try to be a sensible person living a sensible life. She'd tried to reach for the stars, but all she seemed to do was fall on her face.

She tried to wrap herself more tightly in her coat. Her father would be disgusted with her, she thought, for having such thoughts. "If you get knocked down, pick yourself up," was the kind of thing he always said. "Do what you love. Life's too short for anything else."

But her dreams kept turning to wormwood and gall. Maybe she truly didn't know what she was doing. Maybe she would spend the rest of her life failing and falling and being a fool if she didn't turn back from her big plans, her grandiose schemes.

She sighed, shivering with the cold. Never before had she felt so disheartened. Pearce's treachery, coming so soon on the heels of Michael's, shook her sense of confidence to its core. Although she was not usually given to doubts, now she was full of them, almost undone by them.

She obviously had no judgment about men. Perhaps she had no judgment whatsoever, no common sense at all. How could she succeed at anything? Why didn't she just move back to Minnesota where she belonged and teach school or work in an office? Everything she had dreamed of must look silly and frivolous to a rational eye.

The sun came out from behind a cloud, bathing the streets in golden light. The morning's gloom fled, and suddenly the Quarter seemed a place of magic again, a place where anything might happen.

Suddenly some of the shadows fell away from Mollie's heart, as well. She understood that as foolish as it might seem to some, she had to go back to New York and stay there, even if it held few promises for her. She might wait tables and be the voice of a germ, but it was what she had to do.

The street entertainers no longer looked sad or ridiculous to her. They seemed a special, gallant breed, living by their wits and skills. If she had been a musician, a juggler, an artist with chalk instead of an actress, she wondered, would she be like the entertainers here, playing to the nearly empty Christmas streets? And she knew the answer. Yes, she would. She would take her chances, just as they did.

She was a sister under the skin to all of them; performing was in her blood, in the very marrow cells of her bones, and she could no more change that about herself than she could change being right-handed or her height.

A pigeon strutted past her, its brown feathers gleaming in the morning sun. It cocked its head at her so comically that she was reminded of Parvis the cartoon pigeon, the character on the Saturday morning children's cartoons. She'd always loved Parvis the Pigeon. Michael had frequently told her she was silly, wasting her time watching cartoons, but she'd still loved them and kept right on watching them. So what if Parvis the Pigeon wasn't Shakespeare, she'd teased Michael. He was still a delightful character, a classic in his own right.

A wave of strange wonderment swept over Mollie as she watched the real pigeon. Parvis the cartoon character was a TAS production. He must have been one of Pearce's creations. He *had* to be, she thought with a rush of recognition. He had Pearce's skewed sense of humor, a style that could only come from a man like Pearce.

Then, mixing with the surge of wonder came one of dismay. Pearce had said that she could no more help being the way she was than he could keep from being what he was.

Hadn't she ever studied for a part? he'd asked. She had. She'd had the lead as the deaf girl in a summer stock production of *Children of a Lesser God* back in Minnesota.

She'd driven her family to distraction trying to live her life as a deaf person. She'd stuffed her ears with cotton, she'd lived for a week in self-imposed silence, and it hadn't mattered to her that it had been an inconvenience to others. She'd done what she had to do.

So had Pearce. He hadn't lied to her for spite, or for any reason other than to better understand a character he was creating. And he'd told the truth when he'd said she wouldn't have accepted his help if she'd known he could see.

He really had tried to talk to her, to explain—twice. But the first time Irina had interfered, and the second time Mollie had been upset about Fritz. He *was* right. She'd practically begged him to keep any more upsetting news from her because it was Christmas.

I judged him as if he was Michael, she thought in confusion. *But he's not like Michael. He's not like Michael at all. He's like me.*

Suddenly she wanted to see Pearce again. She wanted to stare into his eyes and discover what really lay in them. She wondered if he'd meant what he'd said, that he was only interested in her voice.

He wouldn't have spent the night in the streets searching for her, would he, if he had wanted nothing more than her voice? Hadn't she felt more and more strongly as time passed that something special was happening be-

tween them? And now, because of anger and misunderstanding and stubbornness, they were letting it slip away
from them.

She pushed her cup away and quickly rose from the
table. She looked down the street in the direction of
Pearce's hotel. She began to hurry down the sidewalk,
hoping she would find him somewhere along Bourbon
Street.

But he was no longer in the restaurant where she had
left him, and the tall bartender with the sleeve garter only
shrugged when she asked where the green-eyed man had
gone.

She made her way breathlessly to the hotel where she
and Pearce had stayed and inquired about him at the
desk. He had checked out, the desk clerk said, almost an
hour ago. He had taken a cab and gone.

She paused, staring around the opulent lobby in distraction. There was a telephone booth in one corner, an
old-fashioned one of highly polished walnut, orna-
mented with brass.

She ducked into it and opened the phone book. She
glanced at her watch. How long had it been since she'd
seen Pearce? An hour and a half? Two hours? What time
did the veterinary say he would be in? Ten o'clock? It was
well past ten now. She dialed his office number with
shaking hands. The only answer she got was from an answering machine.

She hung up and looked up Broussard's home phone
number. Again she dialed. A woman answered and
sounded displeased when Mollie asked for Dr. Broussard. "He's with the children," she said. "We're opening Christmas presents with their grandparents. It *is* a
holiday, you know."

"Please," Mollie begged. "It's an emergency. I'll only take a minute of his time. I promise. I swear it."

The woman, obviously displeased, agreed to call him to the phone.

"Yes?" said Dr. Broussard's deep southern voice.

"I—this is Mollie Randall," she said, trying to marshall her thoughts. "I was in your office yesterday with a man named Goddard. About a Seeing Eye dog."

"Yes?" he repeated, waiting for her to get to the point.

"Have they... has he picked up the dog?" she asked.

"Yes. Earlier this morning. He said they were heading toward the airport. Is something wrong?"

"No, no," Mollie said hastily. "It's... there's nothing wrong. But the dog—is the dog all right? Please tell me."

"The dog will be fine," Broussard said with weary patience. "He has some good years left in him as long as he keeps getting his shots."

"Thank you. Thank you very much," Mollie said, then added, "And merry Christmas to you and your family."

"The same to you, miss," he said, but there seemed little genuine feeling in his voice.

Mollie hung up the phone, flooded with relief that Fritz would be all right. But how could she find Pearce? she thought in despair. Perhaps he was already at the airport, already on his plane. She dialed for a cab to take her to the airport. It seemed to take forever to come.

She checked all the gates that had flights departing for Los Angeles. He was at none of them. There was no sign anywhere of a tall man with a dog.

Dejected, she went to her own gate. She had half hoped to see him waiting for her, searching for her as she had searched for him.

But he was not there.

SHE FLEW BACK TO NEW YORK alone. She moved into a room so small that all its furniture seemed crammed together, leaving only the narrowest of paths to traverse. She got back her part-time job waiting tables at Greene's. She did the voice of the germ in the education videos.

She got an excellent part in an off-off-Broadway revival of Tennessee Williams's *Suddenly Last Summer.* She did a commercial in which she played a housewife enthusiastically extolling the virtues of an air freshener.

She heard from college friends that Michael got married on Valentine's Day. She didn't think much about him. Instead she thought about Pearce. She'd given him her address and phone number, and Clytie's, as well. He knew how to get in touch with her, she kept telling herself.

But he didn't. Perhaps he thought she'd meant all those things she'd said to him when they parted—that she didn't wish to see him again, that she would never work with him. She gathered all her courage and tried to call him in Los Angeles. His number was not listed.

Maybe he didn't call her simply because he wasn't interested, and she was fooling herself. He hadn't felt anything special for her. She was someone he'd briefly found amusing, then had decided was too much trouble.

She wrote a carefully phrased letter to him, saying she was sorry she had probably overreacted, and she kept wondering how Fritz was. Had he recovered? How was the mole movie coming? She was just wondering, she said, that was all. She sent it to him care of Thomas Animation Studios with a note to please forward it.

It did not come back. But he didn't answer it. She had no way of knowing if the letter had ever reached him or not.

Spring began to make its way into the city, feebly and uncertainly. Mollie did another commercial, this one for toilet tissue. The Williams's play closed and she got a minor but regular job on a weekly public radio show that specialized in comedy skits.

She bought a tiny black-and-white television set to keep up with what was happening in the world of television. But it was only the children's cartoon shows every Saturday morning that captured her full attention. Sure enough, there were always revivals of Parvis the Pigeon, and Pearce's name was always on the best of them as director and sometimes as writer.

One Saturday, the first really fine, warm one of the year, she sat curled up on the couch, reading a script and half-heartedly watching an episode of "Teenage Mutant Ninja Turtles." Clytie was going to stop by because she was going to Connecticut for two weeks and wanted Mollie to take care of her parrot. Somehow it was always Mollie who Clytie talked into caring for the parrot, and it was a perfectly horrible bird.

Clytie arrived just as the Teenage Mutant Ninja Turtles concluded their weekly adventure with victorious cries of "Cowabunga." The parrot was sulky because Clytie had covered his cage against the spring breezes. He was a very neurotic parrot, and had picked all the feathers off his chest so he was partially bald.

"Here, dear, I have to run, I'm in a no-parking zone, they'll tow me away. Don't let Scooter sit in a draft. His sunflower seeds are in this bag. Oh, and a man stopped by my office yesterday afternoon. He asked me to give you this. I told him I'd see you this morning."

She thrust a flat, white cardboard box into Mollie's hands.

"Who was he?" Mollie started to ask, but Scooter began to scream so raucously he drowned her out.

"Isn't that cute?" Clytie said, covering his cage again to quiet him. "He knows I'm going and he misses his mommy. Goodbye, dear," she said to Mollie. "Don't forget your audition for the pancake syrup people."

She kissed Mollie's cheek and darted off. Mollie shook her head and locked the door again. Scooter grumbled sinisterly in his cage. He was one of those embarrassing parrots who could swear, and he was doing so now.

Mollie smiled to herself. On last night's radio show she had played the part of an absentminded vampire. Next week she had an audition to test for the part of a bottle of syrup in a commercial. She was not wildly excited about dressing up in a giant syrup costume, but the pay was good and Clytie had said they wanted an actress who could be perky.

"Yesterday a vampire, next week perky syrup," she said philosophically. "In the meantime, marooned with a bald parrot."

She opened the large flat white cardboard box Clytie had given her.

Her heart stopped beating. She literally felt it stop, then start again with a painful lurch. Inside the box nestled a red sequined mask trimmed with black feathers; it was the one from New Orleans.

In the corner of the box was a smaller box, a jeweler's box of gray velvet. She picked it up and opened it. Her garnet ring gleamed in the warm sunlight. She drew in her breath sharply.

There was also a large white envelope with her name inscribed on it with a flourish. She set down the boxes, and with her fingers shaking slightly, opened the envelope.

There was a funny picture of a mole. The mole wore a very formal-looking overcoat and a derby hat set at a dignified angle. Dark glasses covered his eyes and his hands were clasped as if in distraction. Every line of his body bespoke lovesickness. A note was written beside him. It said:

Mink—I miss you—Mole. If you feel the same way meet me at noon Saturday at the Mardi Gras Restaurant.

"Oh," Mollie said, her heart thudding. She looked at her watch. It was half-past eleven. She knew the Mardi Gras Restaurant—it was blocks away. If she left immediately and was lucky catching a cab, she might almost make it on time.

She was hardly dressed for a fancy restaurant. She had on an oversize orange sweater, her oldest tights and orange running shoes. She glanced in the mirror. She had no makeup on except a dash of pale orange lipstick, and her hair was loose, but she didn't care. She grabbed her purse and raced out the door.

Behind her, Scooter cursed her roundly for leaving him alone *and* covered.

She arrived at the Mardi Gras Restaurant at twenty minutes after twelve. It was in an old brick building that had been garnished with the same kind of iron grillwork typical of the French Quarter.

The restaurant had a tiny courtyard walled in by bricks that were covered with vines. Several small marble-topped tables filled the courtyard. There was a fountain splashing water down into a pool and a pink-blossomed flowering tree in the corner.

It was there, beside the fountain, that she saw Pearce. Again she had the frightening sensation that her heart had stopped completely, then miraculously but painfully it started again.

He sat watching her, his long legs stretched before him, his elbow on the table, his whole attitude almost casual. He wore dark slacks and a long-sleeved cotton sweater the deep green color of jade. The sun shone down on his brown hair, glittering. Fritz sat at his side, on a regular leash. He looked more grizzled than ever, but when he saw Mollie, he gave one dignified wag of his tail.

Pearce stood as she entered the courtyard through the opened iron gates. He was extremely tanned and fit looking, but his face was solemn. When she reached his side, he stared down at her somberly. "I was starting to think you weren't coming."

She kept careful control of her voice. "I—I had trouble finding a cab," she said. "I didn't get your note until almost noon. Clytie was running a little late."

He nodded, still looking serious. "I see. I tried to get hold of you yesterday afternoon. But Clytie said you were off being a vampire. And last night I had to wine and dine some potential investors."

"I see," she said. Oh, she thought, she had wished so fervently to see him for so long, why did it suddenly seem so difficult for them to talk?

"Investors—for the mole movie?" she managed to say.

"Yeah," he said, nodding again. "The mole movie. Won't you sit down? Have a drink? Something to eat?"

"Oh," she said. "That would be lovely. Yes. Thanks."

As he drew out her chair, his arm brushed hers and they both started at the contact. Mollie felt as if a lightning bolt had jolted through her veins.

"So what's in your future?" he asked. "More vampires?"

She shook her head. "No. I'm going to be syrup. Maybe. On television. If I'm lucky."

"Syrup," he said thoughtfully, nodding to himself again. "I see you on TV sometimes." He shook his head. "You're always talking about household odors. You hold up this can of stuff and talk about garlic and fish."

She shrugged and tried to smile. "It's a living," she said. "I got to be dramatic about the quality of Lingle's Toilet Paper, too."

"Yes," he said wryly, a shade of his old derision returning. "I've seen that, too. A very fine piece of work, that."

He drummed his fingers absently on the table's marble top. "So have you changed your mind? Do you want to be the voice of my mink? Or will your syrup commitments get in the way?"

So that was it, Mollie thought. He still wanted her voice, that was all. The brightness of the day seemed to dim, although the sun shone down exactly the same as it had a moment before.

"Yes," she said, looking away from him. "I suppose I could be your mink." She stared at the cast-iron statue of a frog in the courtyard's corner. She wished she could be made all of metal, like the frog, and have no feelings.

"Good," he said. "Good." Silence settled between them, like an obtrusive third person at the table. A waiter came, mercifully, and asked for their drink orders. Pearce ordered two glasses of wine and Mollie continued to stare at the iron frog.

She clenched her hands together tightly in her lap. "So how's the movie coming?" she asked. She allowed herself to steal a look at him. He was watching her with such fixity she found it disconcerting. It was as if his green eyes could pierce through her and see all the tumbled feelings she was hiding.

"I've got it written. I've got it storyboarded. I've got a studio. Over in west Hollywood." For the first time he really smiled. He glanced up at the sky as if somebody up there shared a private joke with him. "I've begged, borrowed and cajoled enough money out of people to end up being twelve million dollars in debt." He gave a dry laugh of rueful amusement.

"Twelve million," Mollie breathed in awe. "Oh, Pearce—you're staking twelve million on this?"

His grin stayed wry. "More like thirteen and three-quarters. My uncle left me some. I'd saved everything I could. It's all going to the mole. Crazy, huh?"

She shook her head emphatically, and his smile died as he watched her hair shimmer and spark in the sun. The strange intensity had come back into his face.

"I don't think it's crazy," she said earnestly. "I think it's brave and wonderful. I've watched your work—the things you used to do on television. I think you'll make a wonderful mole movie."

"Did I ever tell you that I love your hair?" he asked, his voice husky. "The first time I opened my eyes and saw you, I couldn't get over it."

The remark was so unexpected she could think of nothing to say. She could only stare into his face, trying to understand the enigmatic set of his lips.

"I still can't get over it," he said, reaching over and taking a strand between his fingers. "Maybe I never will. Can you forgive me for what happened in New Orleans?"

Her eyes met his. "I forgave you long ago. I forgave you on Christmas Day."

"You what?" he said, his hand still caressing her hair.

"I understood how it probably happened," she said.

Her voice, usually so well controlled, shook with the urgency to tell him. "It was a series of accidents, what happened to us. You didn't mean to hurt me. You didn't want to. I tried to find you. You were gone. I looked everywhere."

"Good Lord, Mollie," he said, drawing her chair closer to his and putting his arm around her shoulders. "If I'd known that..." He put his free hand in her hair again, lacing his fingers through it. "If I'd known that..."

He sighed in exasperation and didn't finish the sentence. "I wish you'd written to me, phoned, let me know."

"I couldn't find your phone number," she said. "I sent a letter to you in care of TAS. I didn't know if you'd received it or not."

"I never saw it," he said, taking her face between his hands. "But TAS doesn't seem to be forwarding any of my mail. I think Irina throws it away. I thought you'd be like her and never want to see me again. I thought you had every reason to hate me."

"I had no reason to hate you," she said. "None. Just the opposite."

He bent his face closer to hers, the line of his mouth going tense. "Are you saying what I think you're saying?"

His hands against her face filled her with such tumult that her lips trembled. She told the truth because it was not in her nature to lie and what she felt was too powerful for her to conceal.

"Yes," she said shakily. "I think I'm saying what you think I'm saying. I never spent three days like that...with anyone. I never spent an hour like that with anyone."

"Me, either," he said. "Never with anyone but you." He bent his face closer to hers and kissed her, long and lingering. He drew back from her and gave her a crooked smile. "Stand up," he said, "and let's do this right. We were pretty good at it, as I recall."

"What?" Mollie asked in confusion. "Where?" He led her to the flowering tree in the far corner of the courtyard. It was one of the rather scraggly, struggling-to-survive New York trees, but it was just large enough to shelter them from the view of people at other tables.

He took her into his arms and smiled down at her. "I told myself this could never happen. I told myself it wouldn't happen. I told myself I'd forgot you. That you were just a woman, like any other. But you're not. You're like no other. You know, I can remember every minute of those three days. Every word you said and exactly how you said it."

"I know," she said, tears trembling in her eyes. "Me, too. I can remember everything."

He drew her closer, resting his cheek against her hair. "I think I love you, Mink."

"I think I love you, too, Mole," she said, and snuggled her face against the solid warmth of his chest.

"I don't have much money," he said solemnly. "And Mollie, that's the truth. It's all in the movie. I can't offer you much that way. Not now."

"I don't need much that way," she said, winding her arms around his neck.

"Well, someday you'll have it, if everything goes well. I'll hang diamonds on every lovely inch of your body. If the gamble pays off. But I'm taking a terrible risk."

"It's not a terrible risk," she said, reaching up and touching his chin where the cuts had been at Christmas. One had left a tiny scar, and she knew she would love that scar for the rest of her life. "It's a great risk. I *like* risks."

He laughed. "This is a heck of a time to ask a woman to share my life. When I'm just getting ready to gamble almost fourteen million dollars on a mole."

"But he's the most wonderful mole in the history of the universe," she said, and kissed his chin. "You told me so yourself."

"You're one of a kind, Mink. You believe in dreams."

"Oh, Pearce," she said, smiling up at him again, "how did it all happen this way? How did finding each other at the wrong time turn out to be the right time? How did so many mistakes add up to something so right?"

He shook his head, his white grin lighting up his face. "I don't know. Maybe the angels know. If we get to heaven we can ask them. Maybe it was destined."

"Maybe it was," she said happily.

"And Mollie, together, I think we're going to do just that—get to heaven. We'll know every kind of heaven there is. Starting here. Starting now."

He kissed her again, and once more Mollie had the feeling that the rest of the world went away and the only real things left were Pearce, wonderful Pearce, and being held in his arms. When his mouth touched hers, she felt as if their souls were mingling, and her body nestled yearningly against his.

"There's something we forgot to say that last day," he whispered against her lips. "Merry Christmas, Mollie. Merry Christmas, Mink. Merry Christmas, love."

"Merry Christmas," she said and raised her mouth to his again.

The pink petals of the flowering tree stirred in the wind. Pearce drew Mollie more tightly to him, laughed and gave her another kiss. "And Happy New Year," he said.

On the warm cobblestones of the courtyard, beside their deserted table, Fritz ignored them and slept, snoring in the sun. His stomach gurgled slightly.

His tail wagged once, as if he were having a happy dream, and his black nose twitched, as if he were smelling a whole feast of rich scents from the enchanted streets of New Orleans.

HARLEQUIN
Romance

A Christmas tradition...

Imagine spending Christmas in New
Orleans with a blind stranger and his aged
guide dog—when you're supposed to be
there on your honeymoon!
#3163 Every Kind of Heaven
by Bethany Campbell

Imagine spending Christmas with a man
you once "married"—in a mock ceremony
at the age of eight!
#3166 The Forgetful Bride
by Debbie Macomber

Available in December 1991, wherever
Harlequin books are sold.

RXM